A New
BEGINNING

A New BEGINNING

DEWEY RAYMOND

A NEW BEGINNING

iUniverse books may be ordered through booksellers or by contacting:

iUniverse
1663 Liberty Drive
Bloomington, IN 47403
www.iuniverse.com
1-800-Authors (1-800-288-4677)

ISBN: 978-1-5320-4998-9 (sc)
ISBN: 978-1-5320-4999-6 (e)

Print information available on the last page.

iUniverse rev. date: 07/13/2018

CHAPTER
ONE

GETTING STARTED

T HE YEAR WAS 2087 and three young men named Tom Raytheon, Kyle Harkness, and Max Graymore were graduating MIT at the age of eighteen as tri-valedictorians. Along with them were another 200 friends and companions. Tom, Kyle, and Max had formulated a plan for restructuring the earth and ultimately space itself. These men, and quite a few others that they know knew of the plan and wanted to be part of it. The prime circle was Tom, Kyle, and Max. There were nine other young men that all live in the same vicinity and had known each other for years. The first part of the plan was to get enough cash to set things up in order. Kyle was a mechanical genius and was instrumental in getting the plan to take off. He did this by taking a plain metal detector and reworked it to where all it would find would be mostly gold.

Believing he was successful, the 12 of us, along with my mom and dad sat down and discussed the best way to do this. We decided to load my dad's truck with groceries and four ice chests filled with bottles of water. People in the plan had to agree to give up liquor. My mom had a van that held seven people plus the driver. I had one just like it. There were some hills out from Barstow that had once been gold mines, that was our target. We each bought several sets of overalls and mining equipment, plus any other thing that we wanted to take with us. We decided to caravan with my dad in the lead in his pickup and pulling a 12-sleeper camper. My mom next with six of us. And then me and my van with myself and Kyle and four others. When we got to Barstow, we went to the assayer's office and bought the rights to the abandoned mines for $1,000.

My dad picked out a dump truck with up to 50,000-pound capacity. He said he would be by later to pick it up. We went up to the mines and found a nice niche for the trailer to sit. The rest of us arrived immediately and began to work on checking out the old mines to see what condition they were in. Dad unhooked the trailer and six of the guys positioned it well. Dad and mom went back to town to pick up the dump truck. Dad could drive anything. While they were gone, we took the detector into the first mine. On an impulse, I had Kyle check the ground of the mine and to our surprise it beeped almost at once. He played across the floor 4 feet by 6 feet was indicated as being gold. We broke out picks and began to chip away at the bedrock until we could see the gold. We chipped the gold into some good size chunks, but they proved to be too heavy for one person to carry. Two at a time, we took the chunks to the front of the mine. By the time we had all the gold in the dump truck, I had estimated that we had about 9,000 pounds of gold which was worth $720 million. It made us think that we just might find enough gold to start the plan. We needed $10 billion to start.

Over the next two weeks we worked a mine a day averaging 9,000 pounds each day of the 15 mines for a total of about $10 billion according to my calculations. Dad had to make three trips loaded with gold to the assayer's office with a total of 135,000 pounds of gold, which was worth $10.8 billion. By the time dad had come back with the check's, he gave them to me. We reattached the trailer to dad's truck and we caravanned back home. All the guys split back to their houses and gathered what they wanted to take with them. I went to the bank and deposited the checks, surprising the bank teller with the amount of the checks. I got credit cards in the name of every one of the guys that had been at the mines and I gave out those credit cards to all the guys to get anything they wanted to. We were on our way.

We booked passage on the Luna express for 11 guys. Max would be staying behind for he had a job to do and there was no one else better prepared to do it. We arrived in the middle of day. We immediately set to our pre-planned jobs. The guys gathered our belongings and took them to the Luna City Hotel and booked 6 rooms and put each person's belongings where they went. Then they went and got outfitted for space suits and would pick them up later in the day. Things had just started, and Kyle and I joined the others into the restaurant. We told them we had secured a 15-man craft, six years old and comfortable enough to last the trip to the asteroid belt. They had a good dinner and then went up to bed. Early the next morning, I signed us out and paid our tab. We went to the spaceship and loaded ourselves. The radio called for us to break free from the docking port and go on our way. It took us a month, but we finally arrived at the asteroid belt.

We immediately set the 12 monitors looking at different areas hoping to hear the bell ring. It was three days before the bell rang. That is not only one screen but seven of them flashing. Kyle had already attached his tractor beam to the first one and we had put it in our 500,000-pound cargo hold. One by one Kyle would grab them and place them in the cargo hold. The 10th was kind of tight until I discovered why. On one side, there was a long white slab which I took off using my laser pistol and the monitor indicated that it was an element not found on the periodic table.

It was a 20-pound piece which fit nicely into our transmuter. I put it up on high for 20 minutes. The bell rang, the door popped open and there were 200 yellow crystals. Having done theoretical work on crystals in the lab, I scooped up 100 of them and had the liquid fuels siphoned back into the tanks. I filled the primary and the backup fuel tanks with the yellow crystals. I put our speed level on 10 and engaged. We were soon out of the asteroid belt and speeding our way to Neptune, it being the nearest. It had only taken one month when it should have taken two years. I knew I was onto something. At the turn of the century it would have taken 10 years to get to the nearest planet. Yes, we were really on to something big.

We docked early going to the assayer's office where we spilled our load onto the conveyor belt which said our cargo was worth $40 billion. I asked the assayer who was the best builder of new design space ships and where he could be located. He pointed to a man at a gate and was told his name was Larry.

Kyle and I went to see the shipbuilder and took my carefully rolled plans for the unique ship. We walked up to him and said, "I was told that you are the best ship builder anywhere. I have plans here for a very unique ship. Take a look and answer me, can you build it?"

After carefully examining the plans, "this is real? Yes, by the look in your eyes, it tells me that you tell the truth; that you really want this ship built. I can do it but it's going cost you. I mean big bucks, it will take a minimum of at least $10 billion."

"Build it and nine more, here is the check as a down payment with enough to cover the others. I know that something this large will be hard to keep quiet for very long, so I am also buying your silence. Answer no question, if that will not do, then send them to see me. The next question is how long it will take to build it?"

The ship builder started to laugh, but quickly cut it off and looked at us and said, "I will have to pull my best mechanics and body men and get new ones to replace them and quite frankly, there are many symbols there that I do not know. You are serious about this?"

"Seriously enough to want 990 more and serious enough that Kyle will be the overseer and put in those strange places and symbols the things that he perfected at MIT, but some of them still need some tinkering. Now, I ask again, how soon?" I said, looking him straight in the eyes."

He squirmed and then said, "with Kyle's help, the first one could be built in about six weeks. How long will you be gone?"

"We should be gone about three months but call me when you have four more finished and ready to fly."

He said, "Done and Done!" And shook hands. Larry said, "I see you want propellant, but only in the reserve fuel containers. Do you know the lift required to get a ship this size flying?"

"That is the moose's problem," I said curtly. I changed subjects by saying it looks like you're about two thirds of the way done I think another two weeks will close it." I went to the site on a daily basis. Our other ten astronauts were relaxing by the pool. The women tried to engage Manuel and the others who greeted them and then turned back to their discussion.

Now it is the time to place the cone on top of the ship and secure it. The ship was now ready for its first manly voyage. I asked Larry, "what would you say to a three-week maiden voyage?"

"It is a unique offer and I must refuse, for I have work to do." Larry said to his second in command," I don't know how he expects to fly that ship with only 12 people." Shaking his head. but he was wrong. For right at the dinner bell, an unscheduled ship applied for and received permission to dock. Once secure, 188 men marched straight to the new ship and disappeared inside. Everyone turned out for the launch of this gigantic ship at seven the next morning. It was a gigantic ship. It was one mile long and half way down there were six, for want of a better term, wings. They were also weapons, but that part we kept secret. There were obvious firing ports all over the ship. We called it the Sporidian 1.

Everyone waited for the blast-off. It never came but the ship rose stately and at 100 feet the main engines came on line just as a show for the people. We disappeared, and the engines shut off. The yellow crystals came on line, and we were at the asteroid belt in four days.

Kyle's coworkers had some idea of what Kyle's inventions were. Lowest down was the antigravity-pads, next were the artificial gravity pads that gave gravity inside the ship when in motion. Next was the transmuter, although it is not his invention. This was followed by the tractor beam, then came the ship to ship transporter and which was also a space to ground transporter device. The full range in distance was not yet known; although I had used it to bring specific items from in the house on earth which dad had placed them there. Then came the cloaking device followed closely by the force fields, used if a hole developed on the ship and to act as windows without glass. Next came the space screens which theoretically used for the protection of the ship in a hostile situation. For inside the ship, Kyle perfected a replicator to handle our nutritional needs and drinks as well as other tasty treats on an individual basis for the members of the crew.

Kyle put others in various places according to the plan and as needed. We had a movie room with over 1000 titles we had a pool and a spa as well as a sauna, in short, everything a man could possibly want. We split the crew into three shifts 70 men on two shifts and 60 on the late shift. But I continually mixed them, letting everybody learn everybody else's job. As well as cockpit duty. Each man had to be able to run the ship by themselves if necessary. It was not a probability, just a possibility.

We had returned from Neptune and set course back to the Luna city. Our cargo holds were full of gold and about 500 pounds of what the computer designated as e–778. I called an old friend of my dad's; his name was General Harris. I had known him almost all my life. I told him, "I have come across an element that is not on the periodic table." He was immediately interested in it. He said, "sure, Tom, I would be glad to look at anything you have. Just park your ship in the backyard—"

"Sorry, General, but things are not quite that easy. However, if you're up to taking a little trip, I can arrange that."

"Okay, Tom, I'll play along. What do you want me to do?"

"Just go outside and stand by your barbecue pit and I'll do the rest. See you in 10 minutes."

"Alice, I'll be back in about an hour or so, I'll be with Tom and Kyle.

10 minutes later the General was standing on his patio next to the BBQ pit, wondering where this was going to go, then suddenly

he was standing in the presence of Tom and Kyle. "General Harris, meet Kyle Harkness, my number one man and Max Clearhaven my other number one man. You will work very closely with Max if I can convince you that I'm not crazy. You are, just returned from the asteroid belt and made a fantastic discovery."

"But, where are we?"

"Take a look out that window which has a blue glow surrounding it."

The general looked and exclaimed, "holy smokes, how did we get here? And what do you want me to do?"

"As I said, you are on board my ship, the Sporidian 1. It's the first of its kind but it will not be the last. As for where we are, we are 350,000 miles beyond the moon, a distance of exactly 700,000 miles. You were brought here by Kyle's transporter beam. We have not yet found out the full distance that the transporter can operate in, but knowing Kyle it won't take long. What I want you to do is, to set up a meeting with the President for me and Kyle. Here is the reason why," and I gave him a copy of the plan to read as we made our way to the bridge, passing 10 of the, comfort areas. He had walked by them and without his ever stopping his reading.

He finished reading and said, "are you out of your mind? What would I use to convince the President to meet with you for the 1st time?" I took his hand and laid some yellow crystals in it. "Just what are these?"

"Those are what are going to get us in to see the President. Those and what you are about to see, shall we walk to the cockpit?" As we walked the general marveled over the structure and the size of the ship. "You don't know the half of it. This ship is 1 mile long and has 6 wings. It has over 200 firing ports, which we will probably never need. It has ten 200-million-ton cargo holds that are right now full of gold." The general's jaw dropped at the sight of so much gold. We reached the cockpit which was luxurious. "General Harris—"when it is just us, call me Frank." "Okay, Frank, why don't you pick up the phone and call your wife and tell her you'll be gone a couple of hours and not to worry, but something monumental has just happened."

He did exactly as I said, adding only, "I love you, Lorraine. Just don't worry, I am in no danger. I will see you very soon. Goodbye love." "All right, now, you start from the beginning and don't leave anything out."

"First Frank I want to show you what this ship can do. We will set power level at 10 and destination Saturn, engage."

"Saturn! It will take years to reach it. But all right, you said engage, so where's the thrust?"

"That is one of the beautiful things about this ship, it goes so fast and you never feel a thing. It uses the gravitic flows of the solar system and these yellow crystals to gravitate with it. It is these yellow crystals that is powering us now. We came upon them on our first trip to the asteroid belt. It was just almost a growth on the side of the asteroid. Acting more on instinct, I took the slice and put it in the transmuter and 20 minutes later 200 of these popped out. Take a look out the port window, Frank, and tell me what you see."

"Why, that is Neptune. Are you telling me these crystals brought us this far, this fast?"

"That is exactly what I am telling you. We have a new President and I really need to see him and have him review the plan; then, if I can, I will get him to take a little trip like this one. If he agrees, then we start upon "A New Beginning" for mankind. If I am wrong, we have lost nothing but a little time." "We reversed course at maximum speed. There's a difference between the speed level and maximum speed. Maximum speed keeps accelerating until it reaches it limit. I hope I have convinced you."

"Tom my boy, I was on my way out, but you have shown me a new way in and I'll take it. I'll call the President when I get home, and we will see, what we will see." Then we shook hands.

A speaker went off "saying, destination arrived".

"Well Frank, you're back at home. Stand on that pad and we will send you back where we picked you up and we will talk to you soon."

My gold asteroids hit the conveyor belts while the present the bedrock was removed, and nothing left but the gold. I had 20.00

million tons of gold with the value of $192 trillion. Kyle just smiled and picked up the red phone and handed it to me."

"Max here, what's up, Tom?"

"The balloon just went up Max. You have bank of $182 trillion to start to work with and should last you until our next voyage which will be very soon, but the ball is rolling. Max, "I said. "Kyle hopes you're doing well and keep a big long leash on this mad dog here," he said smiling. "To A New Beginning for all of us. This is Max out," and the line went dead. I hung up the phone and swatted hands with Kyle and hugged him tightly.

At 9 AM, General. Harris called, "it's on Tom. President Rodriguez would like to know how soon you can get here?"

"Is this fast enough for you Mr. President. and this is Kyle Harkness there is no other mind like his. I sure am glad he's on our side." Kyle and I crossed the room and shook hands with the President.

"If you had appeared five minutes ago you would've frightened a dozen people. Gentlemen be welcome and have a seat. I have read your general plan and the assayer's office called me this morning to report you had turned in $192 trillion worth of gold, he apologizes for the difference in what he had told you earlier as a rock had gotten wedged under one of the springs of one the scales. General Harris told me of your little trip last night. I have cleared my calendar for the day and I am ready to go when you are."

Then let us all stand and I pushed a button on my belt and the four of us disappeared and reappeared on board the bridge of the Sporidian 1. "Welcome Mr. President. To our new home away from home."

"The number one, I know that they know that each ship will bear a number like all the others. Thus, that means there will be more, but the plan did not say how many; perhaps you will fill in that number?"

"That is an easy number to fill, ultimately, I had planned on 10,000 but I will have to have in operation up to 25,000. But Larry is a slave master and he is turning out in sets of 100 and just as long my immediate 9 are done the rest will work itself out. I am very flexible.

The other nine of this set I know to be finished. I am sure you have been briefed, but on just one ship, we brought in $192 trillion in gold. I picked up the phone for Max's office and told him I would be needing 1800 more men. "Do you think that I can have them by Monday?" He told me of course, but I think you are going to want I would say about 50,000 men I will debrief you briefly. So, when we get back I will have nearly 50,000 men ready to start training. A question Mr. President?"

"A curiosity really, but how are you and Kyle going to train nearly 50,000 men in just a few days?"

"Mr. President, it seems that you have forgot about my core group. Besides myself and Kyle and Max of course, we have Scott, Peter, Craig, Stephen, Manuel, José, Richard, Tony, Johnny and Byron, all of which have been trained by Kyle and myself. They are more than capable of training a ship with 50,000 new recruits. But they haven't been exactly waiting for my call, they have been playing a series of games, devised by Kyle which has been pre-conditioned by the simulators. Using notes from Max and talking to the men with them personally has helped me name the 10 co-captains. They should be adequately trained by Friday. Which we plan to depart at that time. I have been informed that the Elite Armed Services has put together quite a list of metals that should be available in the asteroid belt. General Williams doesn't believe that we will be able to fulfill it. But I think we both know that he is wrong. One more thing before we end this meeting and that is your ride in my ship. As soon as you are ready, let me know."

The President picked up the phone and told his secretary to clear his schedule for the next 3 to 5 maybe more days and that the Vice President should be informed and come over shortly and since I will be gone probably 3 to 5 days, and that will make the Vice President, President for that time period. He will be effectively, the President. Any calls he felt that I should answer personally, but just gave him a viable reason and told to call back in 24 hours. I will be unable to take any calls and to just take messages. I called Vice President Herbert Jenkins and told him what the situation is and that he is

President for the next 3 to 5 days, but not to make any comments as to my whereabouts."

"That was a very smooth, Kyle." "You're a very modest man to be so intelligent."

"Thank you, Mr. President. That is how I designed it to be, nobody likes a rough ride."

"I have a package that should have arrived? Could you beam it up?"

"Certainly."

"You may or may not like this, but I am inducting the three of you into the Army. Before you say anything, I want you to know that you will be five-star generals." Max came on the screen, Kyle did a little work, and, holding up the uniform and said, "what is this?" So, the President informed him that he also had been inducted into the Army and that he was a five-star General, one of only five as Frank is being made a five-star general also. But it's important for you to know that your appointment is mostly ceremonial. However, any man in uniform that you choose to do something, will do it immediately, without question. Mostly you will not have to wear the uniform except at state functions."

"I am relieved at your position. It makes mine a lot easier. Now for the good part. If you are ready Mr. President were going to take a ride. Right now, we are orbiting at 375,000 miles beyond the moon; that's how far we transported you. I didn't want to tell you first because it makes some people a little shaky. Our destination will be Pluto. Our speed level will be 10 and the President looked as if he was wanting to grab onto something."

"It's not necessary to hang on to anything Mr. President. We don't have the pressure or G-Force most ships have. We also have artificial gravity which is why you don't see things flying around. Would you like a cup of coffee, sir?"

"I think I could do with something a little stronger, but it is my understanding that your group do not consume either liquor or beer. So, I guess I'll have a cup of coffee with you. We have every coffee from around the world, what will be your pleasure?"

"I have never seen such a variety of coffee and if I guess right the ones at the top are the lighter and milder choices. So, I think this one, Midnight Black, should be for me as I like strong, black, coffee and I am a connoisseur, and anxious to try it. 30 seconds later, he held the cup of coffee in his hand. The aroma is wonderful." He took a sip and then he took a drink. "He said this is the best coffee I have ever tasted; can you tell me the country it comes from?" The computers printed out the name, Kenya. "I wonder what all I will have to trade them for a bag of roasted beans. I can grind it myself, or my gentleman's gentleman would be able to. Now, where were we?"

"I'm glad you like the coffee, sir, but right now we are just passing through the asteroid belt or actually just above the ring of the asteroid's."

"I think it is prudent to tell you that while you selected and got your cup of coffee, we loaded 50 million tons of gold.

"I cannot imagine going so far, and so fast, and never even notice it. On another note General Tom, do you believe there are other crystals?"

"Yes, sir, I do. Maybe not in our solar system but in the second or third we hope to find our treasure. I think the next question is, how long it will take to get there?" We were just passing Saturn. That is something that I am pondering, sir, but given enough thought, I will come up with it." The President had finished his cup of coffee and wanted to try another variety. He selected the Marion Blackberry Supreme. 30 seconds later he was smelling it, drinking in the aroma and smiling greatly. He took a sip and then he took a drink, smiled, and said "oh, my, what a brew! If you give me the phone, I will place orders for each of these coffees right now to be delivered to the White House and billed to me personally."

"Kyle already started that for you, sir. Kyle has an empathic quality to him which is why Kyle rarely makes a bad judgment. Which is another one of the reasons I keep him. Somebody has got to keep me in the straight and narrow." Kyle laughed which spurred the laughter from everybody else, including me.

"Well, gentlemen, I think I have seen enough to know that I have made the correct decision to back your operation and so, I see that Pluto really is just a planetoid and now we should head for home." Nobody is ever going to believe this, so, I'll keep it to myself."

"If you will wait, and know your office is covered for 3 to 5 days, why not come with us? I am anxious to see the third system. By the way I must tell you that the second solar system is absolutely awash in metals. It's all lying there waiting for someone who needs them. I had planned on sending all the ships I have, back to the system two, to satisfy yourself to system number two, but right now, let's break open these four just now. I thought you would like to open the new cluster that was on the gold we have on hand here now." Everything was waiting for us.

"By all means, I would like to see the process. For someone in my position, it is rare to do nothing while everybody else is busy doing something." We went to the transmuter where four bars of rock stood on the table beside the machine. I picked up the first one and placed it in the scanner which authorized it as being, e – 704. I placed it into the transmuter and set it on high for 20 minutes.

In 20 minutes the bell will ring, and the door will pop open and showed them the contents. Just then the bell rang, and the door popped open and outpoured 500 blue crystals. I took the blue crystals and added them to the yellow ones. Then came the e-506, the red ones and e-886, which were the green ones. The President said, "let's see how far and how fast we can go."

Where it had taken eight hours to go from the first system to the second. It took us only four hours to reach the third. There were eight planets in the system and all of them had splotches on them charting, I got in touch with Johnny and told him to send a ship to the third system. I got a sensor readout of the splotches on the various planets. We brought samples of each to my ship. I repeated the process seven more times and that the scanner had designated them as e – 407, the yellow, e- 704 were the blue ones. The next was the e- 506 which were the red crystals. e – 787 were the purple crystals, e – 886 were green crystals, e– 796, and the e- 994 were the white crystals. I'm not sure why I did it, but I took one of each crystal and made a bracelet to wear. I made one for each member of the crew of the President's office.

I put them all in separate bags and went to the fuel containers where I put some of each of them into the main and the secondary fuel chambers and latched them down. We strolled back to the bridge and took our seats. I put the speed level at 10 and destination coordinates for our home solar system. We watched through the view screen as things became a blur and came to a smooth stop six hours later. We passed by the planets as if we were a car on the street passing houses. By the time we came to a stop, I had fashioned bracelets with one of each color of crystal and had each of us put them on. The lethargy that we had been feeling faded and we felt refreshed. I called Max and he teleported into the White House Oval Office and I gave him his bracelet there. The President picked up the other.

"Mister President, I feel that I must tell you that the one of the reasons why I have no lack of crew members is because all of my crew members are homosexuals."

"General Tom, that is if they admission to make but let me ask you one thing, what the hell does it have to do with this project? Because personally I don't give a damn who you sleep with or when or where or why or how. That is a personal matter that I don't expect come up in the future meetings. We were to the splotches.

What had the looked like a large splotch that weighed in at 200 million tons and was given the designation, e- 778. It turned out to be 200 sheets of metal per pound of element. We took the metal, which was surprisingly light, to our firing range clipped it to a hanger, 25 feet away, and the three of us began firing lasers at the metal. When we reeled it back in, there were no holes, dents or scratches anywhere on it. President Rodriguez asked if there was any way to tell how much more of that metal was there. I said, "sure, all you have to do is ask the computer how many of the splotches fit that control number. Seconds later and 1,250 million tons, which should make 8 trillion sheets of metal. All 3' x 5' each."

"I've got to get in touch with the fleet construction immediately."

"Fleet construction, Haggerty here," the man on the line said.

"This is President Rodriguez, Alpha Beta Gamma 029-8372QQZ, you are to cease construction immediately but only until I get back. Is that understood?"

"Yes, sir, your code is verified and voice print matches. Stopping construction immediately," Haggerty said.

"I believe you are correct except for one man but we need to transport back down to my office, all of us," he said. So, we transported down, and he immediately picked up his phone and said, "Max speaking."

"Max, this is Tom, prepare to be transported." Max appeared in the Oval Office as we disappeared off the ship.

"Mabel, send in the commanding officer of the Strategic Armed Forces." The man walked in and shook hands with the President and started to say something, but the President cut him off saying, "I will explain everything to you Frank, but first I want you to meet your own cohorts. This is five-star general Tom Raytheon and five-star general Kyle Harkness and five-star General Max Graymore." Max's mouth moved but I shook my head slightly. You will work very closely with General Max. He is a man of great intelligence and deep thought. He is a man that commands respect."

"Yes sir, I meant no disrespect, but you have to admit you have me in an awkward position."

"Gentlemen, say hello to General Frank Guzman, Commander-in-Chief of all the government forces, except Frank; you will not have control over General Raytheon or his ships." Kyle and I rose and shook hands with the man, there was no hostility or malice in his eyes, but a hardened look was in there. I could work with this man, I thought and almost like an echo of in his mind he heard very faint someone saying, 'me too'. I turned to look at Kyle and he just gave me the slightest nod and a smile. I *knew* it, Kyle had read my mind and I had read his.

The President said, "I think we should table the rest of this for now except for the fact that they have discovered an impervious metal that we can use to coat all of our ships with; as I can tell from the look on your face and General Raytheon's and that of General Harkness, and an understanding to a long-term problem has just realized itself and it means a lot to them to get back to their work. Everybody shook hands with the others but as we were about to beam up to our ship the President said, "General Harris, would you mind staying for a while?"

"Not at all, Mr. President, he turned and shook my hand and I said, "I am sure we will be seeing each other very soon." Kyle, Max and I disappeared.

As soon as we disappeared, General Guzman faced the President and said, "what is it that makes you trust these people?"

"Frank, we've known each other for years and if I trust them, you should be able to trust them, and besides Frank, here, has known him since before he was born. His father retired as a four-star general himself and what I expect from the young man is extraordinary."

"But, sir, it doesn't make any sense. You made three five-star generals, not subject to me and now I seem to be walking around in a dream."

"Not a dream, Frank, if you had seen what I have seen over the last week, you would have to trust them also. Those three men are going to reshape the solar system and then the galaxy and maybe, the universe."

"What will they reshape it with, tinker toys," he said snidely.

"That's enough, Frank, you have seen their giant ships being built even as we speak. They were designed by Kyle and Tom. How can you doubt intellect like that? Yes, they are young. They tell me that the old ship maker rarely sleeps anymore. He just keeps pushing around the clock, for his workers to finish up the ship's. He has hired 100 more workers. Those two have inspired that old man to feel young again. Could you do that? I know I can never have that vibrancy of energy, but they do and what is more the universe has coughed up its secret to them. Relax Frank, you have met, the greatest military leader known to mankind, and he shies away from the post. I'll see you tomorrow." The General left. "Frank what is your take on Tom and Kyle?"

"They are what you see, and they tell no falsehoods. They don't even bend the truth and to my knowledge, never have, even to their parents even if they knew trouble was right around the bend. So, what they say is truth, unvarnished. You can't go wrong when you wager on them."

"Thanks Frank, you can go now, oh, by the way, you are now a five-star General also. Good night."

"That went well, except for that General Guzman." Kyle laughed, and we went to bed. I was up early the next morning I could see the second Sporidian and the silhouettes of the other eight being worked upon. Larry saw me and came down. "Beautiful, is it not? But then you already have one. So, what brings you to me."

"Kyle and I were wondering when the other eight ships would be available?" I asked politely.

Larry smiled and said, "I figured that would be the case, you can have them in three days."

"Thanks Larry, I knew I could count on you." I gave him a check for $50 billion but before I let go of his hand I slipped onto his wrist a bracelet containing one each of the crystals. He said, "thank you, I think I can retire now" he went off chuckling. "Don't be hasty, Larry, the best might yet to be."

Kyle and I had been wearing ours since the day we revealed each of the different colored crystals. I don't know how I knew what order to put them in or even if there is an order, but I did what I felt in my heart and in my mind.

Kyle and I walked back to the hotel and told our guys in the lobby that we will give them their shakedown flights starting in the morning, but you must first have one of these bracelets. You have three days to become great."

After the three days, 1600 troops got off four unscheduled ships. They had been assigned ships by Max including number one. All one had to do was find the assigned ship number. I stood in the door of number two. I stood in the doorway of ship number two in holding the card to match theirs, a large red number two. Meanwhile Kyle stood in the door number three held up a large number three and pointed to the three taped beside the door. Everything was peaceful and orderly.

We had all 10 ships mixed with the first so there would constantly be key figures to go to. We took off quickly and silently and then suddenly disappeared. We reappeared on the far side of the asteroid belt. I left ship number two with Johnny in charge with four more ships accompanying him, ships four, six, and eight, and ten. Their purpose was to find all the metals that the Space Command needed, and to go to system number two if you run out of anything; for there is more metals in system number two than I have ever seen before. Me and the other four ships three, five, seven, and nine, will be going to system number three to pick up the light, impervious metal that came out of one of the blotches. Johnny, I want to take your ships back to system one and deposit everything the Army wanted and then come back to this system three. Everyone took off towards their own tasks.

The third solar system had no life, but it did have 3,000 large splotches covering nearly all the land of the third planet as well as thousands more on the other planets. I had decided to use the tractor beams of each five of the ships to get into a circle and in unison attach the block and the five ships take it up to orbital height. I had Kyle designate one ship as the lead, so that what he did, the other ships did. It's when we had pads in orbit I use the monitor to see if it matched anything we had already. There were plenty of matches for the following colors: yellow, orange, green, blue and red. There were only 500 of each of the purple, the crystal, and the white.

I have the health of the world on my mind.

Kyle said, "the moment the purple, and clear crystals and the white crystals, were fitted into my bracelet and the instant you did Tom, I found my mind unclear for several minutes and then I concentrated on you and I knew I had to get to you right away." I knew what Kyle was thinking, as either of us concentrated on any member of the crew, we knew what *they* were thinking.

Tom, I had a cut on my finger this morning and now it's gone. These crystals are going to open the way to A New Beginning for mankind and if we use them properly, we could change the galaxy. But, he said, "that using them too much will give you a headache, at least for now, I'm sure that will fade." There was a knock on the door.

I answered it and it was Scott, one of the other Generals, they were captains really, but I had made all captains into Generals and their seconds-in-command were Colonels. "Sir, I wanted to let you know that we have sliced and put in the cargo holds all of the crystals by number which the computer supplied. The yellow is e–407, the blue is e- 704, the red is e-308, the green is e-688, the orange is e-949, the purple is e-976, the clear is e-789, and the white is e-994. I directed that the chunks be brought into the transmuter chamber, and thanks should go to Kyle for his new pocket tractor beam. A 1000-pound chunk of each element is now in the chamber in your locked personal quarters. The handheld pocket tractor beam happens to have made loading them easier."

"Thank you, Scott, for a job well done. How much it empty cargo space do we have left?"

"We have all of the ship number 10 and one bulkhead on ship number eight."

"Thanks again, Scott," I said shaking his hand. "By the way, there will be a meeting of all Generals and Colonels in the conference room at 1800 hours tomorrow after we get back."

I picked up the phone and call Max and told him to purchase a new space dock on the moon and build a 100,000-seat attendance hall. Also start construction on a 50,000-bed hotel.

Kyle and I spent a couple of hours making bars of crystals for each ship, on the basis of the computer read out. It was much later when we got to bed, and our lovemaking was such that words cannot describe it. Sleep came later.

I put two crystal bar sets in a little box with these instructions: you are to empty your fuel containers of all crystals and put one of these bar sets in the main and the secondary fuel containers. Since all of you and the ships you were in had a big part in getting them into orbit, I commend you all.

I told all ships to put speed level to 3. With the destination, the asteroid belt in our own solar system. Engage. The speed was beyond imagination and we were at the asteroid belt in 12 hours. I parceled out the little boxes to the rest of the fleet that was already there. On the ship to ship radio I asked, "if there are any questions, transport over to me and I will explain it to you. Since everything must be clear, I want you to be sure of what you are doing and to set speed level at two with destination Mars. Wait for my command." We had only been gone a week, but some major changes had taken place. I found out just how far it got from General Harris on the phone."

"Good, Mars is now the center of operations. Working around the clock, we have used the tractor beam to move an entire forge to Mars under a gigantic air-filled bubble with a vent for the exhaust. All loads will be deposited here. We needed an easy way to move heavy things around. But I think you will like the place. We also moved the newly constructed Tom's Golden Bank. In using the same moving ability, we moved a mint right beside it. As of today, we are going on the gold standard. All old money can be exchanged at any Tom's Golden Bank. Max has put 3% interest on checking accounts and 5% interest on saving accounts which I am sure you already knew. Now it's your turn to tell me what went on this past week?"

I'm afraid my news is a bit more top-secret and will have to wait until we're face-to-face in a sealed room, General. The news that I can give you is that we got all the metals that were requested since there were no quantity requirements we brought 5 million tons of each metal." Bob gasped, and I laughed and continued, "we were also very successful in finding more crystals part of which is classified. Just know that you will be very happy as all the rest of us are. I'm going to call the White House for I have some major news that is ears only. I plan to set the meeting for 7 PM or 2100 hours. All I will say is that you will be astounded. Tom Raytheon, signing off.

I called the President and asked for a meeting tomorrow at 7 PM on a matter of great importance. He said, "of course, should I invite anybody else?"

I told him, "we need the Commander of the joint Chiefs of staff, along with each of those chiefs but I have something special to show you once the others are dismissed."

"Starting to get to know you has been an enlightening experience, so I will look forward to our meeting with great anticipation."

The following evening at exactly 7 pm; Kyle, Max, and myself appeared against the wall. The President said, "welcome Generals with an exceptionally warm welcome to one I've never met but who could only be Max," he said, walking to him with his hand extended and Max shook it as the President said, "I have been wanting to meet you for some time. That was a very nice surprise for me, Tom, but I'm sure there is more to come."

I said, "thank you for the welcome Mr. President, it is warmly received but let's get down to business. Kyle took a device out of his pocket and set it on the desk. The President on the last trip out in the literally few moments before he took off the bell rang. That always signifies something of significance. In this case it certainly was. Kyle walked forward with a piece of metal in his hands. Please assure me your all dead shots because I want each and every one of you to take your blaster and set it on high, that's right, on vaporization and fire at this piece of metal."

"I must protest! Let me bring in a Marine to hold the metal because we cannot afford to lose you Kyle."

"I'm glad you hold me in such high esteem, Mr. President, but in this I'm absolutely sure of myself otherwise I would not be doing it." So, the commander-in-chief with a satisfied look on his face took aim and fired for five seconds and quit with a rather shocked look on his face. He approached the piece of metal and it wasn't even warm. Each one of them tried until they conceded that the piece of metal cannot be hurt.

I then said, "gentlemen I tried that with the guns from my ship and had no greater success. With that applied to your ship's hulls, you will be virtually invulnerable. However, I must tell you that once secured, it cannot be moved I have a piece stuck to the head of my bed that will be there probably forever or at least until my ship is destroyed. I am pretty sure we brought back enough to cover every ship you have in operation and three times more than that."

"How do you know how much it would take to cover one of our ships?" Said General Guzman very snidely.

I smiled and turned to Kyle and he recited the requirements for the destroyers, the cruisers, and the fighters. From a 1-pound piece you get 100 pieces of metal. We brought back 20 million tons of the element that makes it metal. What do you think, General Guzman?"

Grudgingly he said, "that that is a more than generous appraisal. Is there any more?"

I said, "to my knowledge we got all there is to get because we did not want it to fall into the wrong hands."

General Guzman walked over to me and stuck out his hand and said, "General Raytheon, General Harkness, I wish to ask you to excuse my prior behavior as I did not believe you deserve to wear the uniforms. I admit it now, before you all, that I was wrong, and my behavior was disgraceful."

I said, "we take no offense, General because I know how young we are but today I think we earned our positions." And shook hands with him and we both smiled.

The president said, "that must've been hard to do, but increased my respect for you General Guzman. Unless that's all gentlemen you are released. And they filed out.

I said, "Mr. President, this is the other reason for this meeting and I brought out one box of clear and one box of white crystals, 24 in each. Mr. President, these two crystals are by far the strongest of all of the others put together. When you put the crystals together in the position of the strength in this order yellow, blue, red, green, orange, purple, clear, and white on top, even I don't have words to describe it so all I'll say is that we went from the second solar system to our solar system in less than three hours." The President's mouth had dropped open and he quickly closed it.

He said, "not that I don't believe you, but do you have documentation?" I was into my pocket and drew out the ship tape which showed the original starting point and destination as well as the travel time. I'm keeping this very hush-hush, just on a need to know basis. But that's not all that does, Kyle had a cut on his finger this morning and he looked down to check on it and it was gone. Plus, I know you will find it a little hard to believe, but it gives you the power of telepathy which is the main reason I am keeping it very quiet.

So far only me, Kyle, Max, General Harris, and yourself know what they can do and there may still be some powers we don't know about. "I think it might be wise to put the white crystals only in the hospitals even though accidents are down to a minimum, but they still have them. And the hospitals be able to put one of the white crystals either on to their necklace or slipped into their bracelet where they could be kept in the hospital for 24 hours.

99% of the people will be well after that, it is for that 1% just in God's will for them to live or die. If the injuries are not that severe they should be able to pull out of it. So many hospitals have gotten to the point where they don't have enough patients to stay open, they can't afford the cost. Doctors are starting to carry little black bags again and make house calls. They know that theirs' is almost a dying profession. Most doctors have an office but to keep down the spread of infection, the doctor will go see the patient. Surgeries are virtually unheard of anymore. Observations have made us realize that the first thing crystals of this nature do, is end the pain. A man at a construction site fell five stories and was alive and a Doctor happened to be passing by and put a white crystal into his bracelet, if any of us had been there, I think you would have seen it glow. I recommended to the doctor to leave the white one on for 24 hours and also put the crystal one in the bracelet also.

We went back to the third system with 25 ships this time. Once we got there, he started lifting the splotches and carry them to just beyond orbital height. It took five ships to handle the large splotches. They reminded me of a baseball hitting a small pond and breaking apart into the ripples.

CHAPTER

TWO

I T SEEMS THAT my gag order remained in place as I knew that it would. Considering those that I trust knew everything and can be trusted not to tell. I gathered all my Generals and Colonels in the very private conference room on my personal ship. I handed out to each of them one clear and one white crystal. Those seemed unable to control their thoughts and to keep their own thoughts private. Had to surrender their care and yield to the white crystals. So long as the Colonel was able to control his thoughts he was made a General and the General was unable to control his thoughts was demoted to the Colonel position minus the white crystal ring.

There was about 200 of my men who had been doctors that were given valises filled with white and clear crystals who were sent around to the hospitals were giving proper papers identifying them as doctors who were sent to the ICU and the CCU units of the hospital. The most critical ones were given bracelets of the eight crystals, were out of deathwatch within the hour and were given a new lease on life; but this was not done arbitrarily; if the patient was unable to make their own decision the one in charge of that decision was given the proposal for there was really quite a show who chose death, those were given only a clear crystal which would ease their pain until death took them. The resident doctor was given the two crystals with instructions that if the patient chose a new lease on life he was given both crystals for 48 hours and they were out of danger and pain before given to the next eligible person. That was before we knew how much of the others were available to us.

Our central computer was given all the data on the hospitals and the patients that would qualify, but only if they choose to die rather than continue what has been a miserable life, so be it. The doctors were told that they were not to try to persuade the patients to hold the crystals, merely to ask them what they choose life or death and the doctor was honor bound to abide by such wishes.

In the cases where the patient cannot make their own decision and the one who had to power was a son or daughter were encouraged to honor their pleas to die. Those who were merely in deep pain were given just the clear crystal to ease the pain and cure the source of it which took 48 hours. Then the crystal is passed on. Drug users were given the clear crystal for 48 hours and their addiction would vanish. If the reason for their addiction was lack of a job they were turned over to the armed forces and put them in a position best suited for their knowledge and their experience. To the special envoys were imparted with the knowledge that their complete bracelet would allow them to orient on those not in hospitals. The same choice was made to them as it had been to any other. They were also told that while they had their crystals on and they were encouraged **never** to take them off even in the shower for while they had them on they were invulnerable.

To the homeless on the street they were given the card to their local armed forces, not to add to the soldiers but to find out what they were capable of doing and sent to the proper area for their abilities. In the case of whole families, they were given a place to live and given jobs for what they were qualified for and if they had no such qualifications they were encouraged to go back to college and gain the necessary knowledge of what a subject they had always wanted to excel in. Babysitting is free of charge.

To those who said they could not one work to eat, they were escorted to the local recruiting station not to make a soldier but to capitalize on their abilities which made them proud to eat. To the homeless encampments they were moved to proper housing which was abundant in all cities because the Armed Forces had taken over one third of the population into its services and no one was ever turned down. Again, if the problem is drugs or alcohol, these can be cured.

Within a year all the major problems of society had been solved except for crime. I had a core of my men wearing bracelets and waiting to go into space, went to the prisons "and offering them this: either join the armed forces doing the work they were qualified to do or die. Killers and rapists were automatically extinguished. There would be no more prisons and there would be no more crime. This cured itself in no time and a wide billboard campaign saying, "be good or die".

While all this was going on my ships continued to bring the metals that would be turned into the largest space fleet in history.

Solar system two proved to be a gold mine of metals and at our increased speed we can to fill a need in a within the matter of one day. My personal fleet grew to 25 with another 75 under order. Marriage was revamped mostly because one or both work for the military and they would pick up their children and workers was reduced to six hours a day. This made for closer tightknit homes where children could confide in their parents. Utility bills were ended, and all banks closed except for Tom's. The stock market was eradicated and what those that had been the rich were again made workers. All of this made the social programs previously mentioned were the work of Max. He could handle people better than any person I had ever met and why he was so valuable to me, for despite all the other things he did, he found time to gather up my troops because there are millions of us, many of which married to please their families, but most people just don't care.

I asked Larry, "when will the other 25 be ready?" The effects of the bracelet had worked wonders with the older man. "You are now 75 but you move like a man at 40."

"All thanks to you, General Tom, all thanks to you. The new 25 will be ready in a week. I no longer build ships for others, and I tell them I have only one customer. They know who that customer is. I said goodbye to Larry and walked to the new hotel whose only customers are my men. When I got back to my office in the hotel and called Frank and told him I would be needing widespread doctors. They were needed to go back to doctors that paid house calls. Many of the cities had been demolished and returned to food production. Max closed down all of the insurance companies generating a new workforce.

We held a meeting with the doctors 100,000 at a time at which time they were to put on to the patient either a necklace or a bracelet each containing one of each color crystal to leave with them permanently and if they needed more we gave them a phone number to call and a box will appear at the knees.

Many went back to school and learn to do new things. There was a shortage of skilled and unskilled, but learning needed by many according those that were fighting cancer and other debilitating illnesses were now being treated with the complete crystal packs in necklace or bracelet were never to take them off, not even to take a bath.

Then came the manager's, with name charts on all of the 25,000 new men by the end of the month. These days I was bringing my new men earlier than I use to. It allows me to pull men off the ships and let them have luxury suites to themselves in the hotel. I can then move the new men into their slots and they can begin their training. The hotel would handle over 100,000 but it rarely had several thousand in it at one time, but that was about to change.

I went to see Larry and asked him how soon another 100 will be ready? Larry just said, "I can read your mind, boss, and yours too, Kyle and you did see how far along the ships are and should be ready to have them in another five days. I was about to ask Kyle if he would mind going to Larry's to assist in the electronics of the new ship's."

"I want the 25 ships that are ready, and I want the new 100 that a more advanced crew of the 5000, an experienced crew to take over. Once these are ready, I plan to leave five here for security. *Kyle thought to me, I feel the pull of will also. When do we leave.* I responded, "*in 15 minutes or less if I can manage it.*" Our thoughts separated. I only just realized that I had been dictating and mind talking with Kyle at the same time.

I found myself saying, "Then if your ship number appears on your screen and you will be one of the ones staying for security, the rest of the 20 ships will come with me. We formed up and set speed level on five. With full stop at solar system number two for further clarification. Three hours later I said to all ships. This is not an expedition; each ship will accompany me to solar system number three. You are to ascertain if there are any lifeforms on any of the planets and make note if any there are spacefaring. You are to note if any of the planets have the splotches that were found in system three. You are to place cloaked space buoys from end to end.

You are definitely NOT to make first contact. You will have two weeks to analyze your systems. If you do find a splotch on any planet inhabited or not, you are to wait until nighttime over an inhabited area and use your newly enhanced tractor beams to lift not only to orbit but to track all the way to the end of the system where you are to eject a buoy where we will be meeting on the return trip. By all means, new men are to touch nothing unless your instructor approves. It will let me know they are under observation, but they won't know by who, what, when, where, or why. If they are not a spacefaring race note whether they are preindustrial or pre-space. If the planet is uninhabited, still take the same precautions. Are there any questions? Then good hunting and remember to record everything from this moment on. And good spacing. We had dropped off 14 ships one per solar system.

When they came upon solar system 14, the scene of utter destruction was all that were left to investigate. This was a class

M-one planet, so it was safe to get out and explore, which we did. In teams of 10 they took a shuttle to the surface with Kyle and I had agreed, mentally, that this was a good maneuver. It was definitely here and with all 10 shuttles now in the air, we were getting information like destruction but just no people. They look like homes but not only were there no humans, there were no beings of any kind although some showed paintings of the more advanced races. There was plenty of photography, just no photographers.

Some homes had fires still on and they were using natural gas. One thing I forgot to tell you earlier, was that the addition of the clear and the white crystals to your bracelets will eventually make you invisible unless you choose to be visible and no matter what weapon they aim at you, you will be fine. For you will be, for all we know, invulnerable. When you return to this ship at the end of the three weeks you will have to turn in both the crystal and the white crystals, as the white crystals will cause telepathy. But it takes training to learn how to use it best.

In time they will be issued to you permanently. In the yard of one domicile is the remains of three beings they put on air conversion masks which also acted in a medical capacity to filter the air of any disease. There were three bodies in the ship. I said, "do not move anything else. I am coming down there personally. I beamed down as far as them with Kyle, plus, our doctors and genome identification teams. After an hour it was decided they were decidedly reptilian that grew into beings with their own basic body parts although not in the same place and not always that do the same thing we found a tape recorder behind a piece of furniture. Kyle beamed back up to get his universal language emulator. It was powered by what was now being called a "stack" which Kyle referred to a stack of crystals like every fuel tank had.

It took a couple of hours, but Kyle finally worked his magic and we began to understand the language, so we started the tape from the beginning and it read, "I make this tape in the hope that some sentient life form finds a way to transcribe it into their language. We are under attack. We don't know by who or why except that people are not being killed, they are being made to stand in groups and taken up in their landing craft. They smile as my race is being made into slaves and that is happening all over the entire planet we only had a planetary population of 16 million 10 million male and 6 million females. All the children were included but are separated.

Since we do not know where these attackers come from we managed to get off 16 space buoys and containing a pointing device, so you know that this occupation and a very great armada our entire fleet is being made into slaves they are not taking any gold or money of any kind nor metal of any kind, but it may be that they wanted to eliminate my people and move in theirs. All I know is that this is taking place and has been taking place for the last 30 cycles of the moon with there being 30 days to a cycle. "That was less than three years ago, "said Kyle, "and that could mean that they are three months back on their way home with that many slaves it would slow them down tremendously

I said, "I think we should go find them and see how far ahead they are and then go home and regroup. All ship report ready. I want speed level 10 with destination earth. I picked up the wormhole radio. "This is General Tom Raymond calling. "No note. Urgent! Urgent! In need of immediate meeting to review current information of a danger to earth."

We uncloaked and floated right over Washington D. C. With my ship stopped directly above the White House where it was 8 PM. The White House was a flurry. The President buzzed me and asked my position I told him over his house. He said to beam down, I want to talk to you first before the herd gets there. So, Kyle and I beamed directly into the Oval Office where the President waited for us. As soon as we appeared, he walked over and shook both our hands. "Tom, I have great respect for you but what is all this urgency," so I told him about solar system 14 and which had an eerily quiet and that much of it was destroyed probably information from records.

I told him, "I left five ships on their trail and to use Kyle wormhole to get messages to us. We had left a copy of Kyle's translator with them and all men who work specifically with Kyle would be hard at work trying to decipher their language. The president heard for himself the recording that Kyle had salvaged and the deciphered the information. I let the tape role in the president listened to the final hours. As everybody finally arrived I told them the same thing I told the President and let them hear the same radio tape. I then said, "that this could happen so close to home I think we have an obligation to rescue the enslaved people to prove that not all aliens were hostile."

There were the immediate objections from what was now being called the Federation Air Corps. The president called for silence and he got it. The president then said, "I want to know what the smartest man in the room is thinking," and he turned to face Kyle. "General Harkness please explain what we have just seen and heard."

"The hostile race that did this is capable of doing it before and it probably had. Plus, you have to think of the fact that the recording said is going on for nearly 4 years if you think back to our own beginning in space flight. It has only begun in 2035 and space flight at all began in 1962. We started the Industrial Revolution in the year 1804. That is approximately 250 years. The point I'm trying to make is that it would take them, even at warp speed, and if this is not the first time, it is very possible that it took them over 200 years to plan their long-range maneuvers that is by sheer luck that we were overlooked by them since our planetary population was less than 6 million and they were looking for at least 10 million before they would even think about it. Now the one that was left behind I think we have a moral responsibility to rescue these people if we can. I yield the floor to Tom.

I said, "just how many destroyers we have completed, general Guzman?"

General Guzman replied, "we have 50 million destroyers and 25 million light cruisers with each vehicle carrying 35 fighters for a total of 2.6 billion vehicles in the fleet so far. Because we really have the advantage both in our sheer numbers plus the fact that we will have the element of surprise on our side in general Raymond's 50 shapes give us a huge advantage. I don't claim to know how their ships operate but to have general's Tom and Kyle planning this operation in cooperation with my division, I think we have a good chance of freeing those people, regardless of what they look like they are still people. I return the floor to General Tom.

"That pretty much wraps up this meeting, Mister President, I know I launched the urgency too quickly but the thought of those people probably dying drove me crazy that I could not have helped them at that moment, it put me over the top. I apologize, and I think we need to write up the code that defines urgency in our actions. Mister President, I ask you to write up that code." The officers all left, and the President turned to myself and Kyle and said, "why did you not tell me about the white crystals and what they can do? The first wave of telepathy hit me, but I quickly discovered that I can block out all thoughts and had better control to the relevance to me. You'd be surprised at what they are thinking. But now to business I want you to gather as much gold as we can and the next three solar systems in the General was right, you do have 25 new ships that will be ready within two days. Kyle keep up the good work, I don't know what we would do without you. Gentlemen, with my respects, I bid you good night. And Kyle and I disappeared back up to my ship I told all my ships they had a 48-hour break. Captains are instructed to deposit members at their own home if not in the compound they are then instructed to go to the compound for it is the only place that can handle the ships. Most of my crew live in the compound and we will have your others dropped off. Which we did.

I landed at my parents' house and Kyle's family were there, too. After two hours of chitchat I could feel Kyle in my mind saying *we need to break off and go see Larry, this is important. I agree with you my love. I felt mine and Kyle's father both saying take care of business and then we can talk more, Kyle's father agreed.* I said everybody stay here but Kyle and I have about two hours' worth of business that cannot be put off. This ship rose into the air and first we went to see Max. It's always good to see Max and I want to tell you there is a 48-hour R&R going on right now, but first we need to tell you that we are going to need 10,000 men in three days. Do you need more time for it Max?"

Max said, "just 10,000; not a problem I have set up for my call board 328,000 men just waiting and wanting to be called. I will get this started and then I think I will take a little R&R. It's been a while."

"Do you want us to drop you off somewhere?"

"Apparently forgot my last Christmas present which my own private shuttlecraft with a crystal stack was powering it and enough guns to make a destroyer back away. No, I am going to go down to the compound your parents have invited me to come several times and I think I will. I get a good time laughing and talking with her and your father and with Kyle's parents also. Anyway, consider this done they will be there in three days or two if you wish it."

Max said, "okay Kyle you will have to be there in two days' to give you the extra training time." I noticed for the first time that Max wore his stack as a necklace. He had the telepathy down pat. So, we stood up and shook hands and hugs. We beamed back to my ship.

We went to see Larry and asked him, "how many ships he could possibly have for us in, let's say, three months?"

"Something serious has happened, has it not. No need to answer but I can give you 100 more ships by that time and maybe even more than that. In fact, I can guarantee 200 ships. It's really bad, isn't it. But he turned his back to us and we left.

We went down to my parent's place and Max showed up a few minutes later. Dad decided to have a barbecue and let all the neighbors know the meat had been boiling for a couple of hours and on his barbecue grill he could handle all meat at one time. My mother had made a large potato salad and Kyle's mom had boiled up 100 ears of corn which was transferred to the barbecue grill to remain warm. Lots of the guys and their parents came by. Kyle had installed in all the compound houses the food generator. And they were both making good use out of it.

Had not been brought up to date on all spatial matters and the four of them had kept secret of the clear and white crystals. But the two days passed to quickly, but we exchanged hugs and kisses and shook hands with Ken, Kyle's dad. Our fathers promised not to let our mothers in on the mammoth job ahead of us just in case they knew something that we did not. We beamed back up to my ship and you could see the ships rising from all over the compound and back at Luna city 20 minutes after we docked an unscheduled freighter carrying 15,000 men docked in the 15,000 men filed out and went straight to where the giant ships were standing each ship we had, and each had a number on it. Each man had a number and made his way to his ship.

While the men sorted out the ships, Kyle and I went to the fertility clinic and donated enough sperm to bring about 75 boys and 25 girls each. We had decided it was time that we became fathers but, we just didn't want to do it in the traditional way. There were 100 women egg carriers for each of us and we just gave a list of traits that we wanted our children to have without them all being the same. Our parents were ecstatic about the news. It would be four born every month for two years so that they would truly be a family. We built a school in the town area it was also part ranch because they had horses and cows as well as some pigs and ducks and chickens. We built a house for the couple whose son is in the program, they loved it and kept it ducking the clean all the time they were only 55 days old, but we gave each of them a clear and a white crystal inserted in their bracelet or necklace. This would allow them to do what they wanted for a longer period of time. We returned to base before the men on the extended passenger liner pulled up and docked. A few minutes later the men began filing out of the ship and headed to the Sporidians. This lot would give us 50 ships in the in my personal fleet. Kyle stood beside me.

The fleet had been briefed and we were leaving one eighth to patrol home world. We were sending 5 million destroyers and 10 million light cruisers and one billion fighters. Along with all 100 of my ships. All we are waiting for is a signal.

After what seemed like a lifetime, the signal came in knowing that there was an armada, we now had to assess the exact size and number of ships. That would fall to me and my number of ships in my fleet.

CHAPTER
THREE

ME AND MY ships hit speed level 10. It took two days to reach the armada it was enormous but not as large as what I had expected. There were 400 ships surrounding the slave ship. The rest of the fleet were thousand kilometers away, waiting for our signal. I made a line of my ships in front of their ships and called for all halt. They did come to a stop but thanks to Kyle's language translator we were rapidly able to tune to their frequency. The first thing we heard was, "why did you stop our fleet?"

"I stopped your fleet because I have reason to believe that you are hauling slaves and the Armed Forces of the Confederation will not permit it. Surrender your slaves and you can be on your way"."

"Do you think that 50 vehicles are gonna be able to stop us," he said with hideous laughing.

"You can do it willingly or the hard way and these ships are far more than what they look like." Nonetheless they fired the first shot. I had my ships opened fire and we launched our fighters over 25,000 of them.

"He opened the line laughing. To the left of my 35 million fighters monitor I had a screen that pictured all of their ships and the slave ship. I sent Kyle a mental message *I think we should have the fleet move in just close enough to launch their fighters from the rear. At the same time, I think we should annihilate this front row of ships.* Did everyone get all of this?" Yes, was coming out my ears and as one voice telepathically."

With such enthusiasm I launched my 50 ships and General Guzman 3 million destroyers began to pulverize, one by one the enemy ships in my one line fell. By the time the last one fell, "he began to say we surrender. We immediately, with Kyle's help we separated the slave ship from the others. We all called back our fighters to our individual fleets.

Using Kyles language translator, we had them talking in no time.

As it turns out one of our men was a spy. We quickly track him down and it turned out to be Walter Spitzer. Kyle asked him why? All you needed was to come and talk to us. I put you on probation for 90 days. What's more, we were able to prove their home world coordinates as well as the enemy coordinates. We did not move from our location, but I did have, a chance to try and contact General Tom telepathically. *This is Grico to general Tom Raymond, if you hear me, would you please call me and say so?*

"Would Grico Archibald, please come to the main cockpit on ship number one." A few minutes later there was a knock and their stated Grico. "Well, Grico, what so urgently needed to be said in person. If it was the fact that we heard you stand before us then I can tell you, yes, we did. I am not sure how many can do telepathy. But we are going to find out, but right now clear crystals are being given to each and every man. I want to thank you for having the nerve to come up here. I think that is due for a medal. As I opened the chest I found them for bravery and over and above the call of duty. I turned and penned both metals on the man's chest. You are now a Colonel, dismissed."

The remaining raider ships refused to surrender even knowing they did not have the weapons to beat us. It was a hard decision to make but Kyle and I cannot rule on any other operation. I had Kyle set up the triangulation necessary and completely surrounded by ships. I instructed all Generals to set their weapons on disintegration and all of our ships fired into the triangulation until there was nothing left.

I told all of the generals and fleet captains to write up the battle the way they saw and heard it. Kyle and I did the same. I dismissed the fleet and they returned unscathed.

We pulled out at speed level 10. Destination solar system one. When we reached there, I sent all of the ships on a few days of earned R and R, Kyle and I went to the White House. General Harris was already there and was Chief of Staff of the Armed Forces General Christian Denali, too. Kyle and I parked on the south lawn of the White House and beamed directly into the Oval Office. The President started things off by saying, "that was quite a show of force, do you agree General Raymond and General Harkness?"

"It was a successful mission, Mister President, however it did not have the ending I thought that it would, I mean that if I was the one being rescued, I would show a little gratitude, wouldn't you?"

"I certainly would, "said General Guzman, "if it were for lack of white cloth to wave in the air, I can personally attest to that in fact, General Raymond offered them a new planet to call their own, if that was their desire. But they refused to speak about any of it, and their speech was filled with profanity's and they refused to even let him finish a sentence. General Williams do you corroborate this report with your companions?"

"I certainly will," General Harris replied, "General Raymond gave the original fleet, a chance to survive and they wouldn't take it. After disabling their ships and separated from the slave's ship; he asked for the coordinates, but was rebuked, no matter what he offered to them, they refused."

"General Harkness, what was your take on the entire situation, if you please," said Mister President.

"I move that we make it universal that General Raymond's actions were of the highest possible and both the enemy's and who we felt were rescuing, they turned out to be just as mean and vicious as their masters had been. So General Raymond did the only thing left to him, he vaporized them all."

Mister President said, "I move to exonerate General Raymond and General Harkness for what happened a long way away. All agreed on the other hand, "he took the count, "all oppose raise your hands. Then it was so moved that said General's operated within bounds of the law."

"And now for resolution, I resolved that General Raymond and Harkness be made our first contact personnel. All in favor say aye, the ayes have it and the motions are carried. And two weeks of rest and relaxation is granted to the Sporidian fleet, which will have swollen to 500 or so Larry tells me. I hereby end this executive meeting."

Kyle and I meet first up to the Sporidian number one check if they need anything besides me. I rifled through the names in my head and stopped and I said, "well, Derek Konklosian, you have me what would you do with me?"

Derek was well aware of the fact that I had used his full name. He blushed crimson and said, "I was just thinking that, having worked with you for two years and had never seen your face up close. Stupid I know, please forgive me, sir."

"There is nothing to forgive, Derek. Every man is curious about the man they work for especially having been hired by somebody else, like Max, he takes care of many things for me, but this is the most important, and I do not take it lightly. But now you have seen me and have had a few minutes conversation with me is that sufficient for you?"

"It's been going all over the ships, that were telepathic; and this little scene is going to make it balloon," he said smiling. With Derek this was something, if you care to carry it to all the ships, is the fact that I am not telepathic. Kyle and I walked up at the moment you were thinking your thoughts. So that is all it was, just a happy coincidence. But I am happy to have you working for me, Derek. It proved you to have your own mind, and I like that. Keep up the good work," I said as I patted him on the back.

Kyle and I exited out of the door. For as far as you can see there was nothing but Sporidian ships in every direction. Larry came up to us and said, "I didn't want to do it, but it was a five-star general giving me the command. He said I would have a need for them soon. And that you would take care of payment when you saw me."

"You don't have to worry about paying me, for you and Kyle are the brightest stars in the sky and I have already been paid more than I could ever hope to spend in 10 lifetimes. It is an honor and a pleasure to serve you and all that you stand for."

Then I guess you are part of our Confederation?"

"Pardon my ignorance but what is this Confederation?"

"We just finished over the laws and bylaws committee which was not needed to be straightened the document, but this is where we stand. Exactly how many ships do you have ready? Larry, speak to me."

"We have ready for flight 300 ships with another hundred readies in three days and another hundred by the end of the month. The officer did say that I would end up wanting 1,000. And told me to work on them. Please tell me I have not acted stupidly."

"No Larry, you have not acted stupidly at all, but the officer that came to see you will feel the fury of my wrath. One thing that I can ask of you is this, was it a battle cruiser, and did you just happen to see in the numbers from that ship number?"

"It just so happens I saw the numbers 6458 as he boarded the ship."

"It tells me where my loyalties lie and that I know you to speak only the truth. I will stay in touch on this." We disappeared.

I landed in Max's comfortable domicile, but we went to his work outside. "Anything urgent going on Max?"

His assistant was with him and made a motion for secrecy. "Five-star General Tom Raytheon and five-star General Kyle Harkness. And now I'm going to give you a gift and that is that you can take my shuttlecraft. Give us a nice long safely time here, close to an hour. Now take off before I change my mind." He was gone in a flash. "Now, gentlemen, what can I do for you?"

"I have a lot to do, let us go straight to the center. Can you look up a federation battleship from just these four numbers?"

Max slid easily behind his desk, "and punched in lot of numbers, while we waited for numbers, I told Max that he had done Very well for himself." There was a whirring sound and the answer popped out. All it will be waste in the commander. Kyle and I beamed directly on board and in the cockpit. We put on our dress uniforms for the morning mixing. They saluted, and we saluted back.

"I want General Abrams up here and General Guzman." They came though rather reluctantly. I got right to the point, "who gave the order for the additional ships of my design. General Abrams was offered the door and he quickly went through it. General Guzman said, "I gave the order because you are well understaffed."

"Whether I'm overstaffed or understaffed is my business" and "you will take your nose out of it, as we were very well as identically were thinking to get some of your troops" on board my ships. But it will not work for I have sealed all my ships old and new to the new code but my own." There was a tinkling and then the President said, "has it come down to this?"

"Mister President I honor and respect you and your position and would never dare to second guess any of the decisions. I have got to know right now who is in charge of my fleet?"

"Why, you are of course, why would you think differently?"

"Larry's last authorizations from me was for the 200 ships. Today he said, "he said that you told General Cruz see authorization to increase to 500 from the cruiser. The last four numbers Bearing on its authorization to add said that the order. From the ship but that the officer was a five-star general and the assayer only four of us and I know that three of us to not do it that leaves only one."

General Guzman stood up and said, "yes, I did do it but it's only because I think he's not being fair by not having any women on his ships"

"General Guzman I will direct my words to you. There is nothing but men on my ships because we are all homosexuals and women would cause a lot of problems."

The president said, "Frank this one is going to go against you. When you signed up, you promised to obey whatever President was in office, you cannot pick and choose which ones you would listen to and which one you would not. Plus, General Raymond's organization is really a private funded organization and I made them Generals and part of our organization on the proviso that he keeps choose who is on his ships and the ones that are not. I'm afraid this leads to a loss in rank."

"Mister President General Guzman made a mistake, one which I am sure he would ever try do again. He is a master strategist and we may need him in the near future.

"General Raymond you just stood up for the man who tried to be your undoing. Are you still sure you **want** him with us?"

"Yes sir, I do because anybody can make a mistake it's the second one that would be his undoing."

"That the resolution I feel is resolved, now can I get back to my gin game tonight?" I teleported him out to his origination point." General Guzman stood up walked over to me and said, "thank you for my job for it is my life and I am sorry I tried to interfere with yours. He stuck out his hand and said, "maybe we can work together after all."

"I hope so, for I know that there are several of your men that swing both ways depending upon what's available. So, if you were to post on your ships the fact that my ships are run by homosexuals and that if that does not bother them, then we welcome them with open arms."

That very day the posters went up and those that had seen my ships in action and did not care if a hole was a hole. A surprising 650,000 members of his crews wanted to intern our ships and try playing the other way. I took 100 of the ships and put 50 of Guzman's men and one of the ships particularly #201 and with 50 of my seasoned men together and they worked well. At night, they worked very well together. Then he decided that he would make several of the destroyers all male and they worked out.

But as Kyle and I strolled we knew things are not as calm as the seemed. I got a hold of Max and he sent in enough personnel to fill the other 99 ships giving us 300 total ships. I stopped in my tracks and Kyle turned and looked at me and says, "oh! Boy! I have seen that look on your face before. Okay, lay it on me."

"How about if we leave our solar system to the Confederation. We should be able to see 60 solar systems close enough to be trouble, but far enough away this big fleet as it is should be able to handle anything we come across. I reaffirmed that first contact must be made by either me or Kyle." The President, General Guzman, and General Harris all like the idea because we've had been having too much non-action sense the battle."

We were sitting in the Oval Office and since I had had a good night sleep and had gone over my proposal and reject it. I had decided to go two ships per system that would give us 150 that would be the proposal I would suggest in the meeting. So, I suggest we send out the ships to per the discovery of where those men had started, and to know where they had gone or would have gone had I not vaporized them. So, we start two ships per solar system giving us 150 systems to check. The President started to dismiss the meeting and I said, "before we go, General Kyle has something to give thee and since Max is in control of situation I hereby give the floor to Max."

Max materialized and shook everybody's hand; he got right into it. I heard that you are going to leave five of our ships to guard the solar system over the next and the next, etc., but since we have, all filling me in ships and we can leave one of each of the destroyer class to guard each and every sense and giving us 300 of their ships will not en-danger any of our ships but if there is an attack then the rest of the fleet can't respond probably more" quickly than we can. All in favor of my proposal signify saying, "aye" it was unanimous Yeah! General Tom has the floor.

Tom said, "We have always known that a certain percentage had been living a double life when they got married, they knew I could fix it by taking the position the fleet offered with the proviso that his family would be taking care of. Tom himself had made the offer to keep his family well, knowing that he was one person whose word given could not be broken. That same proviso had been given to each of the married men and again began to any destroyers joining my crew with the proviso and each man from the fleet.

It is time also that any member of the fleet that comes to fly with my men are totally and completely paid. There is no pay day. If you have a child, and its birthday is coming up and you want to get a present on his own. All you must do is walk in the shop and bring your purchases to the front, then stand and hand in the card you were given. No muss, no fuss, take your presents home and wrap them up and take them to the party.

Members of the fleet cannot work one day with the fleet and the next was the destroyer group. These things are done in 6-month periods. There is no confusion and there is no arguing or quarrel if your General cannot satisfy the situation, I _will_ through whatever means it takes. Everybody back to work.

I had my own project, which was to set up a travel system between star systems. That way citizens of other species can come and see us in our daily life routine also, people from other species and buy something here and if they like it will be here to take back as much as they have money for. An interstellar shipping line sounded good enough to me to put it into operation. I asked Larry how long it would take to build the ships if we could make it only one half as high and half as wide. Plus, if you remove the beds and put in seats with some of them regular size and ranging in size and bulk. Plus, if they were taking anything back with them, they can easily be stored in the cargo bays. And if there is a large going back to the place's we just kept opening more and more cargo bays. But it is paramount that you have your goods ready to stall and plenty of time to stall it in, because the quartermaster was very pernicious about his time schedules. He does not let them change, either.

Kyle and I went to see Larry, who, it was said, he had been drinking quite a lot.

"I want to thank you for the information. It was quite an enterprise, keeping his garden up out of his thinking about the Sporidian II's. It is time for you to come out of there."

Recognizing my voice, Larry opened the door and came out. Just tell me what you will need, and Kyle and I will make it a point to fix it."

"You, Tom, and you, Kyle I trust. The others I do not formally accept on the reason is that none of these, have any practical experience with this type of ship."

"I will send you 10 of my best men to resolve the problem."

"Done and done" and, Larry, you know what to do when you have a problem. Forget anybody who was, because we are always back every two weeks. If necessary, just press the orange button I will be here within minutes. With it being orange, I know not to take the entire fleet with me. Feel safe, Larry. And with that Kyle and I disappeared."

Time passed, the days turned into weeks, the weeks months and the months into years. Some of my children are 11 and some of them are 12 but I love them all equally. All of them were exceptional, with photographic memories and total to recall. I had some redheaded boys as well as the blondes, brunettes, and the black haired by the dozen. But that doesn't mean that I love my boys any more than I love my girls. The birth mothers and then nannies had been rigidly instructed. They would be home schooled but actually we had the school house on the compound. I made it plain to all my employee's whose children also uses the school were told that each child would be taught what he adapted to best. They got a well-rounded education in all subjects. I had retired teachers beating down my door to be able to say that they had taught at the Sporidian school.

But my children and the others that went there were rigidly taught courtesy, dignity and honor as well as the truth and why it matters so much. They knew the time to be quiet and a time when it was okay to speak your mind. There were 1000 students at this Sporidian school. When I announced the opening of the school even the administrators that I thought would break down the door, became authorized by the state and all of our teachers had won many awards and certificates plus, the teachers had the option of living on the compound. Our children consumed no red meat but a combination of fruits from trees and berries off the vine and all vegetables. Any particular child that said, "I don't like that" was not forced to eat it. But they were all encouraged to try different things.

We are at the end of another R&R vacation and all of the 11 and 12 year-olds were given the opportunity to go into space.

FOUR

W ITH ALL THE petty things gone, it was time that we provide some needed metals for the fleet and some gold for the bank. We had not quite made the conversion complete. I got the form needed for metals from General Guzman. I set 10 ships to do that job and I took 5 ships to get the gold. Both groups of ships went to solar system 2. I've never seen metal in such quantity and in such a variety. We found all the metals that they armed forces had desired along with 30 million tons of gold for the bank.

We were making first contact every few days. Being cloaked, allowed us to explore the systems that has sentient life, and if they are spacefaring or not.

If they were a spacefaring race. We stayed just beyond their orbital and space route that trapped their satellites and if they had space station(s) on the how advanced they were and dedicated to the ideals that were equivalent to ours and wanted to work on obtaining them. Their desire was to find a first contact sentient race, but they did not do it because they knew that always my anger was cold consternation and even more good than yelling at them; just for making contact with another sentient race.

We did our work efficiently noting the species was sentient or not. We also became a more proficient team by learning how to tunes Kyle's language translator. They are not yet aware of us, and I like to keep it that way. Send the planets coordinates to first contact station on Mars. Kyle and I took cloaked fighters to the surface and just above what obviously was the planetary headquarters. Their ships had competently explored the other planets of their solar system and would soon begin interstellar travel. It's true that there are only two other planets, right now.

Kyle, I know you are thinking what I am and that it is this is the time for first contact and I agree with you that they should bring presents to them. They have earned it.

We uncloaked, and all the bells and whistles all went off. At an old but still powerful man clapped his hands and the signal ended. Kyle and I appeared before him and I said, "I am General Tom Raytheon and I am with General Kyle Harkness, we come in peace as resident first contact officers, we greet your King. I give you our greatest gift. The crystal has been set into a ring. Put it on any finger and it will fit and in one of your hours, you will begin to feel better."

The king said, "my name is Arcturus, and I lead the Owinto people and have led them this will be my 75th year. My viceroy will die before I do, and I will be able to name a new viceroy. Who I had always hoped of meeting an alien, now I have done so and can now meet death with open arms, but there is no death in me now." He began to look younger at a faster rate than normal which was a good sign.

Kyle said, "your Majesty, as long as you wear that ring, you will still die but not for many of more of your years. We have watched you for years and know that you are a good monarch. You have been good for your people."

"General Harkness, I have had to be ruthless at times. All too long the people have passed us by; while living on short rations and people will revolt."

Kyle said, "Your Majesty, I think we can help you there, can't we, Tom?"

"Yes, your Majesty. What kind of foodstuffs do your people consume?"

The King sent for a book that listed on what his people consumed. He opened the book and turned it to, Kyle and I, who were now standing beside each other. The king pointed to the first food and said that this is the favorite of my people but comes in short supply."

Kyle and I were quiet for a while, conversing telepathically, then I asked, "what would you say would be a good harvest and shall last 90 of your days?"

"That isn't easy, because a good harvest is 1 million tons."

"This is personal, and you can refuse to answer, but I ask now, what are your current supplies, of this one item?" I asked.

The King blanched as he said, "unfortunately we are nearly out, and the season is already over." He covered his eyes.

Kyle said, "your Majesty what would you say if I could get 250 million tons of this item. It is on its way here now, but I can cancel the order, if you wish. Similar loads of the next 10 items are also on the way. We do not believe you are impoverished, you are like sentient beings all over that eat what others cannot physically handle."

I added, "we are in the process of making first contact with most of the space that we now control. How do you feel now, your Majesty?"

He exclaimed, "why I feel better than I have for more than 50 years! You are sitting there and telling me that this ring is responsible for this?"

Kyle answered, "that is exactly what we're telling you, your Majesty any of your gravely ill people can have one of those rings put on their fingers and within 72 hours they will be well." Without hesitation he said, "take this to La Haca but don't take that one, take this one it is one and the same for your love of LaBoca." I raised my voice and said *stop* with the force they could not understand, but they could not refuse and that surprised even me. "Everybody take your seats and I will explain. We have a limited number of these rings and

I will be back one day to pick these two up, but you can keep them for one year of your time. For they are precious to us. I know the time is not for games but how old you estimate me to be?"

"For one of such power, I know that you are not the sapling you appear to be, I would have to say 40 of your years."

"In reality, I am better than 40 of your years. I have 100 children just as partner, Tom, does. We hope to be going to see them soon."

"Genetically," I spoke up, "there is one little subject that we must discuss; that is the fact that we don't want planets fighting each other. So, you must agree not to form your own space force. Rocket ships to the various planets that you can survive on we will help you obtain as much is possible We will provide all the protection from any enemy that attacks you. I know that there is some grumbling about this, but let me put your minds at rest, I will use the new name: it is the Galactic Space Force. It consists of currently only 25 million battleships with 50 million battle cruisers. Each battleship has 50 fighters, and each cruiser has 30 fighters for a total of over 30 billion fighters. Our fleet is invulnerable." This brought several smiles and a little laughter. "Please have Sporidian. There is nice safe position you can watch this from. Now if you will have your most powerful phaser placed 50 feet in front of the fighter go for burst for as long as you want."

Kyle said, "they are going to try to pull an old trick on you. But the fighters and no damage range and would be any response." "I know my love. "You may fire when ready. It let go a volley of tremendous power for 20 minutes. Emergency response teams, but they were not needed, the pilot got out and bowed to the crowd. Then he stood aside while his vehicle was inspected. It was one of our little secrets we keep in hand.

"In addition to the regular fleet we have our own personal fleet of 1,000 and trust me when I say that one of the ships is equal to 10,000 destroyers. It is late but if you're inclined I would delight you with the insides of our ships." We parked the ship on an abandoned airfield I encouraged my crew to circulate amongst the people for I had made it plain that we can understand their language even without the translator. These people were reptilian, and nature made into sentient creatures and they had come a long way. Yet the spoke English.

Kyle, myself, and the King talked long into the night; about our extended plans to set up both the life form ship and the service between worlds upholding contracts supplying what we need while we supplied what you need. The king thought it was a marvelous idea and the introduction of races could form friendships from system to system. The king asked, "how is that you can travel so fast? We ourselves have broken the warp drive, but it seems nothing when compared to your speeds."

I answered very carefully, "your Majesty, that is one thing that I cannot say. It is the center of our power, and not to mention the inventions that our own Kyle here would not have been possible. I have over 50,000 of the smartest people in the Confederation on my ships working with Kyle to improve future designs of the ships. But it is getting late and I think some sleep would have good results for us all, but before we turn in, you had a cut on your hand would you take a look at it now for me please?"

The king looked at where the cut had been and it was now completely cured and I gave him a box of 25 of the white crystals and told them, "use one on, have your doctors treat those that are near death and if you have enough of them just keeps circulating them as those that is no sickness it will make them well again you can rename your doctors as healers. Now it really is late, and I do have to leave tomorrow but I will leave the 25 fighters. But understand, that they are under our control but if you have any spot of trouble, let the Captain José Ybarra know and he will be happy to handle the situation for you. Now Kyle and I bid you good night. Kyle and I disappeared.

The next day, I gave the King the tour of the ship omitting top-secret areas. He said, "and you and Kyle drew up these plans yourself!?"

I responded, "most of this Kyle mostly figured out, but then again the plan itself was of from me." The King just walked around talking to himself, "amazing, just amazing" I had the other four ships land

and we spent a couple of hours using our replicators to make a bunch of their delicacies by the thousands. There were two ships assigned to this large continent and one to each of the other continents, so that no one got left out but, by mid-day, it was time for us to leave.

On one last question, the king asked me, "how do they fly? When you have no thrust?"

I said before closing the door, "your Majesty, that will just have to be another question that cannot be answered. One last from me before we go, "your Majesty, I was wondering if ever you fish with the line and pole?"

"I haven't since I was a young man, why do you ask?"

"When I head back this way, I plan to have a few planetary leaders come together with me to one of the most scenic sites ever seen and has some of the largest fish that are very tasty. Think it over, and I'll ask you again when we comeback by."

With knowledge of the first contact situation I called the President and he was very interested to hear the outcome of the meeting. After the meeting, we flew to Luna and I went to see Larry and told him I would like him to make 10,000 of the ships minus the weaponry and all of Kyle's editions except for the transporter and the replicator. He said it would be no problem and an honor to do it for me.

After that, we went to the Oval Office. Invisible now, we materialized when the last man had left the office. A meeting with the President, General Cruz, General Kyle, Max, and myself. It is always soothing to see Max. The President wanted to know how the first contact situation went about and the longer I spoke, the bigger smile he got. They accept the fact that they would not have their own space army but mollified by the size and scope of it. Kyle went over, and he put in a logical feeling that they had a thing that they who seek with no always told him someday not now, but someday. He approved leaving 25 of the fighters on guard and they were pleased by the placing of the red button which would bring the entire space force. I asked Max what the situation was in really personnel.

Max said, "you have 3 ½ million ready personnel. I want to know if you have cracked the telepathy operation."

"Max offered to come give any help you need and give General Cruz some personal help in making the investment. All left for discussion. We think shook hands all around we all disappeared as the next will be the R&R. Personal R&R which pleased the entire crew Kyle and I disappeared for a while and we returned I told my mother as Kyle told his that they were be grandparents. We each will have 100 children each born and months apart. Which was a cause for great celebration, but as always, we eschewed the alcoholic beverages.

The next morning, all the talk was about the babies. The first set of babies in fact the first one gave me more time to get ready for the second set sure was not there…then I recovered and turned around and went back to make sure that my firstborn will come out as Tom Junior the medical turned around and went racing & to be sure Kyle's first born was a Susan. On this I did have a glass of champagne.

Each child born will have an ETM, or electronic tracking module and we were turning out one to three children each month until it turned out that I have 84 boys, one set of quadruplets, and 16 girls. Kyle had 92 boys and 8 girls with 3 girls being triplets.

CHAPTER
FIVE

T HE YEARS WENT by, but I would not allow the kids on any of the ships during a mission, but the children were allowed to go with the passengers/cargo ships that were now in line. I had 33 members on my fishing expeditions out of 60 first contacts. But many of those I think wanted to. But even on those that did not, they didn't have very influential members of their society and arrange the transport to come to their systems also. Since everyone used a different currency control enforced by food crops but we introduced the Tractor from international Harvester, J. I. Case, and John Deere and they were all able to increase their crops nearly 50-fold. It was one of the strings we had to pull but carefully. With my careful pulling we got their planets on board with the Confederation of planets. It was a stern warning across our 200 planets that they were not to touch, what they did not know what the primary power supply is, and the one on the other side was the secondary power supply. But their power stacks included only the yellow, orange, red, blue, and purple. No clear and no white rings this. We were just now introducing the rock rake used to get rock from a potential field.

This was to be followed by the Rototiller and made the soil a little easier to work with. Next came the power again, this time to make rows for their crop.

Since many of the worlds had no population many of the world's we serviced put in agreements to settle their people because of overpopulation. It was then that the most, strange thing happened. This farmer came to me, it was a rule that I was not be bothered, but I waved them away and went to sit beside the young man. "Just what is your problem but first what is your name?"

"My name is easy for I am Lan Tou and you are the venerated one, who all others say should not be disturbed by anyone. I am sorry, and I will go now."

I called out to Lan Tou, "they will not bother us again, now I ask you one more time, what is your problem?"

"Just answer the question," this time it was Kyle. Kyle and I had coalesced the moment we felt the problem.

Knowing he was speaking to the two most knowledgeable men on the planet, he gathered his will and said, "there is an area of land that we would like to farm but there's a huge mass covering three quarters of the total land mass."

"Hold still for a minute while I think this out". *Kyle and I switched to telepathy and I said that can only be 1 that I missed.* Kyle said to the young man, "we will have to go immediately. Tell the king our pardons." Kyle smiled just as I did, and he brought his latest invention, his pocket transponder. He played it on the mass and it was actually two masses there the larger one was white and the other was clear. I walked toward my ship to the site and used their tractor beams to grab the first mass and then again for the second mass each time being raised to orbit height I sliced some of them into slabs to my cargo hold on the ship you put the remainder of the white and all the clear crystal and put in Kyle's ship. Then I took the balance of my five ships plus, five others chosen at chosen at will the very best men for the largest load of gold ever.

Kyle said "I'm sorry to interrupt you but I was the only one who could. That fifth ship had only 15 million tons of gold."

I said, "it doesn't matter, it is still largest load of gold ever assembled.

"I switched the count already to read one billion six hundred million tons of gold. Kyle, as always, you show up in time. You went into my mind and saw there was a little trouble. So, I took the balance of joining the two groups of ships." We went to the mint only to find a much-expanded project. The bank was now a monster of a building and you will always want to see this enormous building. We went outside to find Max, which was pretty easily done. Max didn't waste time on preliminaries, cut straight to the bone.

"It was a deep space buoy wasn't it?"

"Yes, from very deep space number 1154."

Kyle said, "if they are coming here, unless they have improved the technology it will take them 10 years to reach us, and that protection accounts for a 50% increase in the technology. I did not inform anybody else but came straight to you."

"Thank you, Kyle" I said, "you did right in bringing it to me first. There's no need to alarm the others at this point. Although several telepaths may have gotten a trace before I shut it down. Kyle it's funny that if I shut off a telepathic wavelength, it is shut off on all the others. What do you think?"

After giving it much thought, Kyle said, "I think that is because he was the first one to hold and keep it on them ever since. But that is just my take on the subject." And he smiled at me. I suddenly sat up right and asked Kyle, "did you feel that?"

"I felt it, Tom I wonder how many others felt it?"

"I don't think they had much time because I shut it off just as I received it. But that probably means, that the deep space buoy has probably been destroyed and what's more they now know that somebody is waiting for them somewhere down the line." A door opened, and a man entered carrying a tray and set the tray down but did not leave. "Alfred, please leave the room, and shut the door." Kyle started to say something; and held up my hand and I crossed my brow and put my finger to his lips.

I took out his hand and held it with a feeling of growing and swelling until we encompassed the entire ship. We floated in silence until we heard a voice that said, "I don't think they suspected anything. I did exactly as you told me to do. Wait, there's someone with me" taking over that line I told the recipients not to expect anyone with knowledge from this line. It is eternally severed, and I cut the line. Kyle and I coalesced where Alfred was. He was certainly looking at us but could not believe his eyes. "Believe it Alfred. But don't think that just thinking about it will make it happen, it takes years in the long practice to support for Kyle and myself and take these grueling, the sleepless hours, and the infinite patience and both of our deep knowledge to be able to accomplish this and now, because of your treason, it has threatened life as we have come to know it; and for what, what can they possibly offer you to commit treason?"

"It was for my little girl. She is not getting any better with the crystals on her. They said they could cure her in just a little snap. I did it for her."

"Why did you not bring her to us? Bring her forth now **** they brought her in. Her legs were atrophied I put a clear crystal ring on one hand and a white one of the other. Within 48 hours her legs were well. The interrogation of Alfred you told him little that they did not know. We had caught him before and he had broadcast again this time at our urging. From it we were able to get the coordinates of the fleet and moving towards us. Alfred disabused any further contact with them now that he had his daughter back, but we told that he had to play ball with us. We needed a little bit more information. Joined in link with Kyle we managed to get the information on the size of the armada being sent against us and more importantly the coordinates of the planet that initiated the armada.

We turned Alfred loose after he had finished. What we wanted him to do for us. We turned on the colored lights on each ship, so bright and did not need a telescope to see them at night. We decided to move to Mars. The 11,000 ships that I had ordered were fully functional and Kyle supplied the troops for them. To cut down on break in time Scott, Johnny, Alex, Steve, José, Manuel, Peter, Craig, Frank, Spiroc, Tony, and Walter plus, another 81 men joined them in training, but still was not going as fast as I want. So, I had another man join the training core. It went quickly enough to suit me. We then turned Alfred loose with a mind lock.

We were teaching only 10,000 of the ships. The other 1000 ships were training the ships to be sent to be the inaugural of ships carrying people and produce and anything they thought they might could sell or trade. My men were training the men that would operate those who would fly them.

We met with President Rodriguez. Both Kyle and I shook hands with the President and each stood to greet Max with a bear hug and a heavy shake of the hand, and an unusually warm greeting from General Cruz, and the usual good-natured handshake. Now the niceties have been performed, I got down to business.

"Mr. President can I speak?" "General Tom has the floor." "Gentlemen as you are all aware one of our very deep space buoys sent its signal and was destroyed by the armada. Our long-range relay telescope, using the coordinates of the armada as provided by Alfred. We managed to get a blowup of one of the bridge people, as I passed them around, we can see that they are reptilian but in what we call the human configuration. The buoy continued to sending information to its destruction. It seems as though the armada Either to not have warp drive or else just conserving energy using star drive for standard space. There are no jump gates anywhere in this vicinity.

"The armada itself is in in-line travel so you don't know the loot or slaves or both." General Cruz has floor.

The general said, "and I believe we should go forward in mass before they can assume a battle posture and I believe that just the Sporidians could do it with ease. And I would like to captain one of the ships, by the leave of Tom and Kyle." Gen. Kyle has the floor."

Kyle suggested, "I agree with General Cruz except that I think we should go for fuel and weapons. We need to at least try for some peace between us." Gen. Harris has the floor.

"I agree with what Kyle said, we should make some effort to get to know these people before to destroy them." The president has the floor.

"General Raytheon, how long before they reach our space?"

"Unless I am mistaken, they will have switched entry to their warp engines. In which case they could be here within a month."

"General Harkness I agree with your approach but should still go for weapons and fuel, but if you cannot broker a peace, then do what you have to do."

"I vote for the plan with everyone else. This session is closed."

As we left, General Cruz, asked, "if I could have a ride around with the two of you for maybe a week." Kyle and I acknowledge our agreement. "I just want to get the feel of one of them."

"Get what you want to take with you, and Kyle and I will personally show you around." General Cruz got his stuff together and was back on the pad an hour later. We picked him up as we swept by. The General had had the standard tour. But this is more in depth. He found that some things that he knew with great meaning, some they did not. Whatever Kyle and I did, he would say, "show me".

He was a quick learner, but he would get so into it, to get so enthralled, either because he was not paying attention, but Kyle and I recognized the signs had been forced to take him to safe place. Just kept walking around saying, "this is the most amazing ship!"

Kyle looked down and noticed the General did not have a white crystal. Kyle inserted one into his bracelet and the general's signs lifted, in fact, he could not even remember anything before but with the help of the white crystal his dementia was considerably better control. We had one for everyone, but I guess sometimes, somebody is going to slide through the cracks. Cruz had forgotten the simple pleasures of life. But that seemed to be lifting. I guess it just takes longer than others. Especially when they are older. The President showed me the personnel file on Cruz.

He had come from humble beginnings but now he had enough medals on his chest. Then I noted it, General Cruz was 102 years old. But now that he had a white crystal, it would take a few weeks for he to regain himself. We reassigned him to the ship on my right. I told Johnny and Scott that I want him in the pilot's chair. A little resentful but nothing to worry about. I would make it up to them later.

It had been decided that my 20,000 Sporidians under cloak, would surround the entire area. Then if I felt the need, call in the full fleet. General Cruz just wanted to see one of the ships in action. Not that I can really blame him, for they are the most beautiful ships ever built. They are deadlier than any other yet found. It's sheer size! Nowhere had a ship like this planned and indeed made one!

I gave the signal that put us in attack formation. We let go of the colored lights and disappeared. We were, of course, cloaked but it's the waiting that gets to you. Since we had little knowledge of what we wish to find, I asked, "Kyle exactly what he did know.

"According to the carbon dating, this writing is over 12,000 years old and many of the diagram and figures all seem to have dealt with that time. But what little we had, I read. I felt Kyle's thoughts and emotions and I linked with him in the timeless beauty of the fifth dimension.

I was up early and put on the ship to ship and broadcast that if anyone even remotely knew about that area of space, to contact me directly. No matter how many times I looked at it, I was still no further along the road to understanding it.

CHAPTER
SIX

I HAD TAKEN THE ship off speed level 10 and put us down to level 3. I didn't want any neutrino's flying around. If you know what you should be looking for, you can avoid it. And a cloaked ship can be seen as a ripple in space caused by the neutrino's. 20,000 of them could do untold damage. Kyle called to me with his mind.

I woke up refreshed and dressed, Kyle awoke suddenly and said I'll be with you in a minute. Together we left our quarters and headed straight to the cockpit. I put the monitor on long range we started to get a glimpse of the enemy. I set up a barrier of my ships, 10 to the line, and 10 lines, 600 per level and four levels surrounding the ship's. Me and Kyle in my ship and Max with general Cruz in the ship to the right, all still cloaked.

The ships were so small, but that was just comparison. They really were quite small ships, when taking in the aspect. I tried talking to them, uncloaked and, "I tell you now that this area is off limits to you."

"I don't remember you being made my captain so take the big ship out of here before I destroy it."

"I was afraid you would take this line up things, so I brought some help. All ships de-cloak, which they did. Now how about 20,000 reasons to leave here and never come back?"

"If I leave here I better be dead because if I'm not they will sure kill me. Are you up for deals?"

"What did you have in mind?"

"Let me take my ships to sector 628."

"Now, what is so special about sector 628. Oh, that's right Kyle, you gave it to me last night. Have any other deals in mind?"

He suddenly said, "fire at will!"

I let his barrage go on for 20 minutes and I called him and said, "are you ready to give up?"

"I can't give up!" Said Davis, "they would kill me."

"Perhaps you can start something new. I have at least 20 planets with your atmosphere that are unoccupied and would make fine farmland. Plus, you would be under the protection of the United Federation of planets space force. And that is a reason for life. And that is not just these 20,000 ships. I am a welcoming squad but believe me when I tell you I have great power and can do many great things. How many women do you have amongst your crews?"

"We have only 5,000,000 men and 500,000 women."

"I do not see your problem, wherever we are if there are more men than women; we do not take wives with each of our men given a number and if they did not become impregnated by the first man, she would have the number of the second try out. In the meantime, what's wrong with men having sex with men, in fact, it is a gift to not have to have a woman can't get pregnant. When man sex is there, you just wait until your time comes up to become a father. And if you can truthfully tell me that no two men have never gotten together for sex when their women were tied up? If they are all lying to each other and to themselves, because when a man finds an outlet he will go many times based upon his schedule."

"We should talk this over." While waiting for them I researched our volumes on planets with that atmosphere. The worst they could think was that you got destroyed in the fire fight. One of my ships, ship number 19912 to commanding General Raytheon. I responded immediately, General Raytheon responding awaiting report. Thank you all for having to be a part of this. I turned my attention to the members on the screen and asked them if they had reached a resolution yet?"

"That's what took so long, since there is too many with our atmosphere and the idea of owning something for ourselves, so we have decided to take you up on your offer. My name, in your language is Frank Le Gue. I heard right when they called you General Raytheon?"

"You heard it right. I am a Five-Star General capable to over 1 million things, but I specialize in first contact with alien civilizations."

"I can see why, when you can turn a band of raiders into a group of colonials. It will be good to be away from all this killing. How I have hated to do it. Now a new life" he sat up and said, "how are we gonna be able to turn a planet not just for building supplies but also for food."

"When it comes to food, we can help you with that for as long as this phase in takes." I muted up our lines and addressed General Cruz. "You have done one magnificent job without ever firing a shot. It's the bigness of the ships that daunts them. I don't claim to know the numbers of the crew on a ship like this. Which brings to my mind what we are to do for defense for I am sure you will not let them keep our ships."

"You are right in that you cannot have all of your ships back, but it will be some but necessary, we believe you can have can ten ships for you will come under the protection of the Star Force. Which has never lost an engagement, and you will have no need for space-based weapons. The 10 ships we leave for you to go about the system as needed."

"It will just take a little time, but again how are we going to turn this into farm land, none of us knows anything about land and what you do to it to make it growing things. My name in your language, is David.""

"We have all kinds of fancy equipment and there's a large core of men dedicated to teaching how to run this property properly. They have no time limit in which remain." A runner came up to me and stuck a note in my hand the runner waited until he got my answer and then he took off again."

There are over 10,000 ships outside waiting for you to tell them where to unload. Whether fortunately or no, you are the First President even if not wanting it, you can call for elections. At that time, you may find that you enjoy it. Time reveals all."

"We are probably going to need living spaces first, so I found a great spot for the lumber."

"Mr. President I don't think you have a proper notion on just what the capacity of one of the ships is. One ship is capable of shipping over 10 million tons of building material. Want to change spot right over here," I pointed out on the map."

"I think I'm beginning to understand your abilities somewhat better. What else you have?" I told him to stay online while I was online. After returning, I said, "we have got 100 freighters full of farm equipment. We have a crew over at the ancient dam and are optimistic and being able to get energy from that source. My crew is working on it even as we speak. We walked outdoors to the planner and he started going over plans. "Like one or if you like all they are all available. What's more teacher people how to use the equipment and all of this is no charge."

We got everything unloaded and the engineers should have power to the town in another hour. That hour passed like it was nothing. Our craftsmen had 20— 500 bed houses ready to be moved into. Electricity was run to the houses and a water main from the lake to the housing complex so that there was running water and soon will have hot water.

Beds and appliances were moved in including a stereo which startled David. Once the surprise was over he wanted to listen to some of our music and picked a CD at random and I showed him where to put it in. The music pleased him but only half as much as the recording process did.

These people have never slept on a mattress, on the floor and was even more amazed to see it put a frame with a headboard that matched the furniture in the room. Soon, a five-course meal lay before us. We were drinking water and David wanted to know if we used anything stronger?

"No, we do not it affects the senses too much in a bad area of the brain."

They had to be physically coached on the simplest of details, although they pick them up rather quickly and taught others so that when it came time for bed, they slept with new dreams and the ability to make them come true. At the end of the most pleasant day they can ever remember, Kyle and I said, "it is time for us to go, David, but we will fly in from time to time. Then we vanished.

I called the White House secretary. She said, "he was expecting your call which she put right through. "Tom, a pleasure to hear your voice, General Guzman has been in meetings and is just finishing up his last one and should be here in about 15 minutes."

"That should work out just fine we should be there right about then we are here to pick up General Harris on the way. We had all gathered shook hands and all the normal stuff, we got down to business. The President said, "I would say that General the General Raytheon should have the floor first."

I said, "thank you Mr. President. As you already know the situation did not finalize in a fiery conclusion. This time I was lucky, and these people were looking for a way out. I provided the sensitivities as they jumped on them like a pack of dogs. This has taught me one thing and that is fighting doesn't settle anything but talking can. I talked to many of them and they were excited to have their own planet and to know that they would have protection. You give a person what they want and what they need, and they will be your friend. These new friends have provided a lot of information on the enemies. And I did mean enemies. It will take about a year for them to find out that we settled without a fight. This is going to worry the top dogs. Each group sent out now will contain a hard-core group designed to keep them together. They've got to know your fighting strength before they can attack. I yielded the floor to Kyle.

Kyle said, "my observations pretty well mirror General Raytheon's. I talked to dozens and dozens of people who had been nearly at war and suddenly find themselves having to organize a new planet. They are looking to us for extreme help especially in setting up a democratic system, I told them we were to provide that assistance, even if I have to do it myself. I yield the floor to General Cruz."

"It was one of the most amazing scenes I've ever seen in a wartime history. Tom was right, he could sense both their dislike of the fighting and that oozing warm feeling of a way out and a way of finding their own way without being commanded. They are knowing freedom for their first time and they like it. I also spoke with over 100 people and many of them are doctors they don't know what a lawyer is, but they will find out in time. He told them that we had dozens of men to set them on the right course of being a democratic planet of freedom and all, but they also knew they would have to work. Hard and long to find the right people to start you off right, and Kyle and I moved into his slot and I told them that they were in no better hands than that of General's Raytheon and Harkness. You definitely picked the right man to be our first contact liaison it was almost as if he was born into it. I had experienced this for once in my life since I am about to retire."

Tom immediately said, "you already have that bracelet that you were sent?"

"Nah, superstitious bullshit. He looked around to everyone and said are you serious, this really works?" He took it out of his pocket and put it onto his wrist.

I said, "you will start to feel better in 48 hours and by the end of the week you should feel like your old self returning. Then you can decide whether if you really want to retire. Just so you won't know I want you to guess my age."

"That's easy," said the General "you can't be more than 18 or 19 years old."

I was laughing in a full belly laugh. "General, I am 34 as is Kyle and I believe our President is now 70 and General Harris is in the low one hundred's.

The General looked astonished. I'll be talking to you in two days'

The President said this meeting is over and Tom, I would love to attend one of your family picnics with my family."

"The more the merrier, and picking up about five tomorrow, if that is convenient with you?

"That will be convenient for me I will wrap up any meetings and clear my calendar for two weeks. I called for a total of 5 but it will be twenty, I wish I could be more specific."

"Even if you bring 100 it will be okay to us. My mother will welcome you all. My dad will love the opportunity to sit and talk with the President, but I promise sir, that I will not make you weary of him. A privilege that is granted very few and it will be for just an hour or day but two whole weeks!

My mother greeted General Cruz and family as if they had been lost, but had come back home now. She was so graceful, it just came natural to her and she was the perfect hostess she greeted everyone with genuine affection. I told the President that I had surprised my parents when I was eight years old. They were both on the couch and I climbed in the middle of them, turned to my dad and asked him, "dad what is a homosexual?" Knowing that I only ask questions for information I decided to go ahead and tackle the subject myself. I explained to him that two men get together as a couple just like me and your mother are a couple. Being homosexual it is just another form of being normal. There are hundreds of millions that practice it. Nor does interrupt a marriage. If it was my advice I would tell the girls that I am a homosexual but that I loved her but only in one way. For sex I would rather have the man. Does this help you out?

"Yes dad, it did. Along with all my research of the subject and your unbiased opinion I have reason to tell you that I am a homosexual. I have been having sexual relations with the teenage boys in the area. I hope this does not hurt you. I just wanted to get it up to the open so that I don't have to sneak around or go to places that I do not really like to go. If I meet a nice boy I would like to be able to bring him home. I have had sex in several places that I really did not feel comfortable so; Do I have your permission? To bring my male friends over?"

"Tom, you are an unusual child because you have a child's body and a man's mind. I accept your opinion we only have a couple of objections. If I look at a man in his eyes and then I will know whether he can hurt you or not. So, I guess we are giving our permission. I gave my dad a hug and I gave mom a hug, but there was a tear in her eye. So, I will invite him to dinner, of course you can look him over for your opinion because I value it. I got get off the couch and stopped at the doors as I told mom that I will have children, probably a lot of them because I like kids, but I don't think I'll have any until I turn 29. My mother smiled, and everything was okay. This made both my parents laugh. As well Kyle's parents who were sitting across from, Kyle and I who were unconsciously holding hands.

Kyle and I saw all our children together. About how they were doing in school, the things that they wish to be after graduation. They liked it best when Kyle and I would collaborate on our stories which we did telepathically, so the kids knew nothing at all about it except on the last day I held each one close and gave them a kiss and told them that I miss them too but my work was very necessary which they would understand when they came to be adults. I have hugged my oldest son last, and as I did I heard him in my mind saying all the things he cannot put into words. We broke, and I said to him, "you are going to go very far."

Then we said goodbye to the parents, wished us well and good luck in all of our endeavors. We thank them for being our parents and then we disappeared. I had built a secondary compound and now all the men and their families lived in the compound so there was nobody to be dropped off except with the President, who said he had some of best times of his life. We went to the White House and dropped him off. Then the red light flashed, and I picked up the tape come from it, it was still nearly 1300 systems away, so we had plenty of planning time. I dispatched 1000 of the Sporidian ships to the frontier where the long-range buoy had picked up a signal.

All, of course, which will be cloaked, I called for a man named Norman and asked if he had seen any action as yet.

"No sir, but just being on the ship is an experience and I think you for it."

"Norman you going to lead this fact-finding mission. When you reach step one, I want you to take 500 of the Sporidian's and the ships will follow the signal. If you see the signs of the armada, stay with them as they travel so that I may know the speed they travel. Speed safe and sure and come back to us.

We went back to our duties of first contact which led us to system 57. We received a new signal from the earth. It seems that there was a young man from one of the other planet systems who wanted to join the Confederation forces, in particular the Sporidian's. His name is Ishtak Volmr I told them to go-ahead and sign him up to be ready for the next mission. But I didn't want to wait that long, so I contacted the Sporidian 20 currently in command of Leon. I requested Leon to go pick up young Ishtak even though he was out of the Santee Republic and was in the form of a man but was clearly, from some amphibious culture. He was to be assigned a trainer either Jack or Dupree. I want to record everything he says or asks as I am sure he will be full of questions but, be sure to show him all of our pleasure devices." Tom out.

Kyle and I proceeded with our mission. They were a space race that they had not yet left their own system. We had a pretty good file on these people who were man shaped and looked just like any other human. They even spoke our language. We took just our ship, cloaked, and went to float above the Emperor's Palace which also housed the Council chambers. The Emperor was very old and frail. When I took his hand to kiss it, I slipped one of the white crystals onto his finger I don't think he was even aware. We walked back to the Council chambers with the Viceroy, Peter Farkas.

He said, "he grows weaker every day. It will be a terrible loss for he guided the Empire for 85 years ascending the throne at the age of 20."

"What would happen if he suddenly got better?" Kyle asked.

Peter's face lit up and he smiled and said, "you slipped him something, didn't you?"

I said, "yes I have to be truthful about this. I slipped on to his finger a ring with the white crystal and I guarantee he'll be up within 72 hours. If he had a strong constitution before, then to could take as little as 24 to 48 hours. Peter directed us into a garden that he said was the Emperor's own garden when I said, "you plan on keeping us here until he gets better or until he dies. I must tell you that we cannot be imprisoned anywhere, at any time". I stood before the first guard and quelled him with my eyes. Have no fear, for we are not evil, we are only different in small ways. If he pulls through this, I will give you a very clear crystal that will severely slow the aging process.

Your agriculture and your artwork are so shockingly close to our world. It is if Leonardo da Vinci had started this new world."

"Leonardo da Vinci, an artist, writer, complex science fiction, excuse me, for you to go well into space. It was the same man that started this planet. We are related."

"Yes, I think we are." Just then there was a ruckus in the Emperor's chamber. He was sitting up and commanding his clothes. I am the Emperor if you do not do what I say you will die." At that, everyone dropped to a knee to his Excellency, Leon the first. Kyle and I bowed to him. After the pomp and circumstance Emperor Leon, Kyle and I went for a walk in his garden. He asked me point blank, "what did you do to me?"

I said, "look at your ring finger, he looked and saw a beautiful ring on his finger. So long as you not take that off, even in your bath that ring will continue to strengthen you and wash the years away. Do you like to fish with the pole, Emperor?"

"Leon let out a long breath, and said, "it has been many years; but in my youth, yes, I did enjoy it. Why did as this particular question?"

"Because your Excellency, every year I gather the leaders of the world and we go on a fishing trip for a week. No servants, we do everything ourselves; including cleaning the fish, cooking and enjoying it and we all pitch in and clean up the mess. Would you be interested?"

"My Viceroy can handle things here for a week and it would be good to get out and mingle with other heads of state, yes, I think I am very interested. Just give me adequate notice."

I replied, "I always try to give at least a month's notice and we will be having one in three months, that should give them time to restore your will on your people. Unless I miss my guess, they will give a jubilee to see you up and about again."

Emperor Leon smiled and said, "I think you could probably be right. I have gauged the amount of problems in your body and I can tell you that nothing is to be able to stop it completely; but that ring should buy you 10 good years maybe more."

"I knew this would not be able to last for a long time, but it is going to last longer than I expected anyway. I am deeply indebted to the truth of the two of you. But I have things to do, and I am certain that there are things that need your attention."

General Tom Raymond and General Kyle Harkness I make you Regents of the realm for as long as I'm alive. So, I will say goodbye for now," and we shook hands and Kyle and I said "sire, is there anything your planet needs immediately?" He talked to his advisors and then said, "they tell me that you are seriously low on this list of metals. You help this?"

"Yes, your highness, we can give us 20 minutes and it will all be here."

"Are you kidding me? How can so much of so many metals, get here so fast?"

I responded, "even as we speak they are overhead, and are asking where you want it put?"

"There is a large area that they should be able to see, have it deposited there. How much of each mental is here?"

"We only brought 4 million tons of each. I am sorry for the small amounts, but I told them to hurry."

"I won't ask how because I am sure you cannot tell me, but we are deeply in debt to you. You have not asked us to join your configuration, but if you have the papers, I will sign them. He did, and we can give net good him his copy. We shook hands and Disappeared.

CHAPTER
SEVEN

MANY YEARS PASSED, and Kyle and I had made first contact with over 300 civilizations. But Kyle could feel my restlessness though there was little I could do about it at the time. Then one night I woke up and Kyle sat up. We felt them in our minds. Kyle said in unison with me, "Johnny and Steve!"

I responded, "yes, the first two to merge. It had been 10 years, but Kyle could sense I was restless. Kyle and I had long reached the speed of random thought and now that Johnny and Steve could merge with each other, they would be able to take over first contact situations; we were free to be explorers again. But first we must take Johnny and Steve with us on the next first contact and let them handle the entire situation. We would soon be at system 655. They are spacefaring but only locally. This was the first system that Kyle and I had ever visited ethereally, and we wondered who the next pair would be.

In the morning, Kyle and I invited Johnny and Steve to have breakfast with us. They were smart enough to know that something was up but equally smart enough not to bring up the subject themselves. We had a fancy breakfast and had finished, when Kyle and I sat back smiling. I could feel Johnny and Steve wondering what was coming, Kyle just nodded his head. Without preamble I said, "Johnny, Steve, Kyle and I felt you last night, but don't be embarrassed. Kyle and I have enjoyed it for years. We want you to take over first contact situations.

"It's easy enough and the two of you will be going with Kyle and I first contact situation here in system 655. If the two of you work out well you will be elevated to four-star generals, which really doesn't mean much except for status." The two of them laughed. "But it is a serious position and not wanting to be going into lightly. The primary thing you must remember is that you are dealing with alien personalities, and it doesn't always jive with ours. Kyle and I will be with you physically, and I will handle the introductions and then I will turn control over to the two of you. I must know the fish can swim before I turn it loose. You both know of many powers our ships have and you must be careful not to reveal them however, in a situation like the one we are going into sometimes you have to give prizes for joining the Confederation. The most notable one is the transportation pads, not the antigravity pads, just the transportation ones. And if the monarch is elderly and even frail, you drop to one knee and kiss his hand you slip on one of these white crystal rings on his finger. Here's one for each of you, never take them off. They will be the source of your powers of persuasion. Since two of you think conjointly you must always keep each other on the right path this will become easier in time.

"I know that I have given you a lot to think about in a short period of time. Our new tunics arrived in the middle of the night, so you should be very spit and polish for your meeting with the, I believe a King. Be ready to go by noon. Am I correct in assuming that the two of you can teleport without the machine?"

"Yes, sir, it's only happened in the last few days," said Johnny.

"Just be ready for anything. Remember this, the king has the power to know when he is being lied to, so do not lie. We'll see you on the transport at 12." Johnny and Steve exited. Kyle said, "I think they will do well in the assignment."

At noon, Johnny and Steve joined us and I told him, "I have had you on 4 or five other first contact situations. So, you know how to act, and you know what to say, but be malleable. Go with the flow and if there is a snag become the flow. We have been in this location for 10 days now and know it is the center of government. Teleport down but remain invisible until you see the proper opening."

We teleported down invisibly and could tell by the confusion there was little control. One of the beings said, "King Monash would be furious with all of you if he could only get out of bed again." I nudged Johnny and he spoke out while materializing, "I think I can help you with that." The translator was working perfectly. "If I could see your King I might be able to help him."

"I have Viceroy Sarong, who are you or what are you doing here?"

"My name is Johnny, and this is Steve, we handle the first contact situations of our people. I am a general in the Confederation of Spacefaring Peoples. We would like you to join our Confederation." I could feel it beginning to sour so Kyle nudged Steve into saying, "why not let your monarch decide?"

"NO! Where you came from, go back!" Johnny and Steve picked up my vibes and proceeded towards the King's chamber. They made to stop them, but Johnny and Steve walked right through them. "You cannot stop us, only he can." All said without heat which was important. They entered the king's chamber and went to his bedside. He was elderly but not yet completely frail. As Johnny took his hand, he slipped the ring onto the monarch's hand. The effect was instantaneous.

He sat up and roared, "BRING ME MY CLOTHES! I have a planet to run." He spied Johnny and Steve and said, "who in blazes are you and where did you come from?"

Johnny smoothly slid to the end of the bed with Steve at his side and Steve said, "we represent the Confederation of the free peoples everywhere. We have traveled the galaxy putting together a Confederation of planets that no one would think to come against.

We have that power by ourselves, now we wish to share it with you." I was so proud of Johnny's actions that I momentarily glowed. I chided myself for lack of discipline. Kyle laughed but not verbally. The king was dressed and headed to the Council room.

The moment they saw him in the doorway they fell to one knee. He sat on his throne and said, "what, is all the ruckus going on here?" After he restored order to the chaos, he turned to Johnny and Steve. "I don't know how to thank you for relieving me of my aches and pains I was almost to the point of a welcoming death. But that is passed. So, tell me what it is you can do that we cannot."

Johnny and Steve were careful not to reveal too much, just enough to make him want to join us. He fiddled with the ring, and Johnny quickly told him, "do not to take it off. Not ever, until you are ready to die."

Johnny quickly changed the subject, "your Highness, over the time that we have been observing your planet, we have noticed that you produce high levels of grain, much more that you can use. I know at least 100 planets that could use your excess grains and could be asked to trade grain for something you need to be decided by you. There will be one of our travel ships that would be happy to show you what is available for trade with your grain. I believe your economy was quickly become strong and you would go down in the history books as the Monarch recorded about."

"I see, the harvest will be starting very soon. When would your ship be here?"

"I can put in a call and have one here is less than an hour, if you wish it?"

"By all means, how long will you be around?"

"We can be here for two or three days if this okay with you."

"Absolutely, you are now honored guests. Let's have a feast!" While the king attended to personal matters they were shown to the king's garden. Kyle and I materialized using our power to black out the visual listening devices hidden in the garden. I said, "the two of you are doing marvelously well, but we won't leave you just yet. He just doesn't know he's got two additional dinner guests Johnny and Steve laughed and embraced but quickly broke when I said, "you should not do that here. That's one thing we can never tell in advance, is how good or bad they accept or not, homosexuality. You don't have to worry in this garden, for we have blacked out there visual and listening devices while we are materialized, and I am making sure no one is looking in from any other place and if they placed sensitive listening devices at the door or against the walls it would just get a hum. Is there anything you would like to ask me?"

"It is good to relax the superhuman strength it requires for us to be aware of where you are. This is not as difficult as I was afraid it was going to be, but just knowing that you were with us, gave us the strength we need to do a job right."

"This is actually rather fun," said Steve.

"That, is something you have got to be very guarded about because when you are having a good time it's easy to slip valuable information." I asked the two of them, "do you know how to turn off somebody's visual listening devices?"

Johnny replied, "I'm not sure because I've never done it before."

"Well, you can now. I just turned it on in the two of you. That is something you cannot do without."

Johnny shook himself all over and said, "that feels better!" And we all laughed. I felt a hand touch in order and Kyle and I disappeared. The attendant entered and said, "pardon my intrusion but we will be spraying in this area and the king thought you might like to see his art."

Steve said, "I think that would be marvelous, don't you, Johnny?"

Johnny replied, "I love art in all its forms and would be delighted to see yours. I have seen the art of over 1000 planets and it always strikes me strange that no matter how much art I see and no matter who does it, I always get a warm feeling basking in it." They made small talk until we reach the cavernous art room. He served us refreshments and left the room. Johnny trotted out his new power and was delighted to <u>KNOW</u>, that he had been successful. Kyle and I re-materialized and the four of us walked around delighting in the art and sculpture. I asked Johnny, "are you aware that they have tried to give knockout drops to the two of you?"

Steve said, "we were aware but had been on the watch for such a situation and neutralized the chemicals. They also tried to kill us, I think in frustration of their failure to be able to monitor us and listen in on conversation."

Johnny said, "I think it will be good for them," and snickered. We all chuckled appreciatively. Johnny and Steve ushered back into the main chamber and it was two seats open one on each side of the king. The king was very blunt about things. He said, "you do have some very strong powers. I know you are aware that we tried to listen in on the conversation were visually what you and the garden and the room of art. I don't suppose you could tell us how you did it? Don't bother to answer because you would not bother to block us out if you did not want to keep your conversation private, but I have a feeling that there's two more of you here. He raised his voice and said, please show yourselves." At that point Kyle and I materialized. "NOW, there is a power I would like to have but I don't suppose that's in the deal."

I said, "your Excellency I present myself and my companion as general Tom Raymond and Gen. Kyle Harkness. You know how it is, you have to train new people before you can turn them loose to do the job themselves. We are also telepathic as well as telekinetic." As I was speaking the king gracious and in two more chairs were placed beside Steve and Johnny's one on each side. We were having stew which one of my favorite foods but not necessarily Kyle's. He will eat it and not complain, and you would never know that he had not had the time of his life. We ate for a while in silence but as we neared the end of the meal, the king addressed me saying general Tom, "what is it like out there?"

So, I said, "if you have got the time, I'm sure Johnny and Steve would show you around one of our spaceships."

"You say spaceships in the plural, how many ships do you have in our system right now?"

"At this time, we have got 10,000 of the ships just like what you see above you. Can see them step out because we have what's called a cloaking device which does just exactly what it says. Kyle and I made the mistake once and had to hold them off for an hour before our backup arrived. But after we had taken out the first 20 ships, they drew off and let us be. But you can imagine their exclamation of so many ships. But the defenses of the Confederation are far more than just my 20,000 ships, we found to keep the peace, you have to be prepared to fight even if that is not your desire will run against two races that refused to concede defeat. When I told them that if they did not surrender, they would be destroyed at stony silence and a renewed vigor and in their attack. So, I had all my ships re-cloak and went away and left them in piece. I posted space buoy telling all of our ships to stay out of the system but when the Emperor stood, his Viceroy put him in prison for failure to do what was best for his people."

"His name was VeJarboe and he became Emperor. He stood in front of the throne and called out for us to materialize, which we did. From that point on, we had the normal first contact routine. He made comment about how little copper they had and 20 minutes later I asked him where he would like it put? Of course, he didn't know what I was talking about and said so. So, I told him that there was this ship hovering above the building with two million tons of copper, where would you like it put? He was flabbergasted but quickly regained control diplomatically and was told to place it near the steel mill. Which we did. From that time on, we had a new friend. Now our freight line makes regular rounds to them in their jumping from system to system. They needed a lot of things and discovering that they could trade off their excess because each one was of value to someone else and they learned you do not have to go to war to obtain things that you need. Sorry to upstage you, Johnny but sometimes I get on a roll and can't help myself."

At which the new Emperor roared with laughter. Johnny said, "Sir, it is a privilege to be upstaged by you." The Emperor said, "you have extreme loyalty in your men, don't you?"

I replied, "it is because I love them, and they know that I love them all and that I would fall on the sword to protect anyone of them, and they know that." We had eaten our way through nine courses but drank only water saying to the VeJarboe that they never touch any alcohol and please do not be offended; it is only because mistakes can be made under the influence of alcohol."

"No offense taken, General. I can tell that you are very able leader. I salute you," and a raised glass and all the others around the table raised their glasses.

Kyle said, "if you will pardon us Emperor VeJarboe, we will leave you in Johnny and Steve's very capable hands, but we have duties elsewhere."

"I quite understand, General Kyle Harkness and I appreciate your acceptance of our being here. This time they will really be on their own." At which point, Kyle and I disappeared. The Emperor had no way of knowing how long of a link I had with Steve and Johnny.

Johnny said, "Emperor, is there any metal that you are needing? Or anything else for that matter."

The Emperor hesitated and said, "I want each of my people's representatives to say that one thing that they know we need." They did as he said with Johnny and Steve noting the item.

Steve said, "it will take about an hour, Your Highness in the meantime I would like to ask you if you like to fish I've noticed your lakes, rivers, streams and oceans, abide with them in the plenty."

"It has been many years, since I held a pole in my hands, but I did enjoy it; why do you ask?

"Tom and Kyle left an extensive list of emperors, presidents, and kings that at least once a year get together on a very beautiful planet that has no population and they go there without servants or food tasters or anybody else to help them; but I have heard that they have the time of their lives because they do things for themselves helping in any way they can in catching, preparing, frying and eating the fish they had caught. But I think it's the freedom from responsibility that they enjoy the most. Can I add you to our list?"

"When will the next one occur?" The Emperor asked apprehensively.

Noting the caution in his voice, Steve said, "in six months, but if you are concerned about the newness of your elevation, we can hold it on your southern continent which is largely unpopulated, why is this?"

"It is because underneath the dirt, there is a large mass that I think has been there before we were sentient. The people believe it is haunted and no matter how crowdly populated the northern hemisphere is, they cling to their superstitions and refuse to go there. Would you mind going with me in my ship to this place?"

"I would be delighted! Regine, you will hold the fort, until I return."

"If you would come and stand between Johnny and myself and we will teleport up to my ship." With a look of delighted surprise, he took the place appointed him and the three of them vanished.

"If for no other reason, this makes your visit a delight," he said as we made our way to the bridge. Johnny took the captain's chair and Steve offered the copilot seat to the Emperor which he happily sat down. "I don't hear any roar of engines, but I'm sure this is one of the things you cannot tell me." But he said it very happily. A few minutes later we were over the spot of the mass. The monitor prodded up on the screen even though it was covered with dirt and grass but just each round had been left exposed. I called five of their ships to me and in a few minutes our tractor beams sliced through the dirt and locked down on to the mass.

The Emperor asked, "what do you call those beams of light?"

Johnny replied, "they are called tractor beams. Once given their coordinates they go through anything else that is there to latch onto their quarry."

The Emperor was surprised that Johnny answered the question but did not press his luck. He just enjoyed the experience. We lifted the mass to orbital height and using laser's, sliced the mass and it was put on board three of the ships. "You have a projector?"

"Yes, we do, why do you ask?" I have made a film of this removal and you can take it and show it to the masses and it should dispel their superstitions." By now, back over the Castle, the three of us beamed down from the transport pads this time.

The Emperor asked, "I don't suppose we could have that little invention?" He had the look of someone who already knew the answer, but Johnny was in contact with me and I told him it would be okay to do so.

When Johnny replied, "I think we can let you have this little invention as it has no military use." The Emperor looked like a man who had Christmas come early. "You will have to show Steve for him to install the pads at and sent for your best engineers and I will instruct them how to build it." A runner had run out and fetched their best engineers. They were both astounded and delighted. A large box materialized and in it were transport pads. "Put these pads anywhere you want to transport to and be explicit in the destination coordinates. Well Emperor the ships have returned with those things that you wanted, and my captains want to know where you want them put."

"What is the quantity of each one?

I said, "there are 2 million tons of each item." The emperors jaw dropped and then got control himself and said, "There is only one space large enough and is easily seen, you can instruct them to put it there." I passed along the coordinates to Johnny and he told them.

We then told some of their best engineers how to make the tractor beam. With Steve supervise the putting of one together. A big box of parts to make tractor beams. "We have only one more thing to do before we leave and that is to sign that you are joining the Confederation and installing a red button on the Emperor's throne. If you are ever threatened by anybody press that button and you will have nearly instantaneous response from my people." The Emperor signed it and Johnny gave to him his copy.

We shook hands all around and Steve and Johnny disappeared.

Johnny and Steve reappeared on the bridge. Kyle asked them what they thought of the experience. Johnny responded first saying, "that was the most difficult thing I have ever done. It is so draining.

I don't how the two of you have done it for this long. 300 times is a miracle, and all of this sprang from your mind sir?"

"Yes, Johnny, this is my grand plan that I worked on for three years while going to college at MIT with Kyle and Max, who help me write it. It was getting started that was the hardest part of this grand adventure. The two of you were fabulous. Congratulations, you and Steve are to move to the Sporidian number two." With the flick of a couple of switches and every man on every ship. He told them all that Johnny and Steve were taking over the fleet except for the 1000 ships I am taking with me, check your monitor in the bridge for yes, you are coming with me. Intercom off."

Since I had placed buoys only up to system 1000 I resolved to start there and see what happens. When the 1000 ships had acknowledged that they were going with us, we pulled away from the fleet and disappeared. After a month we had mapped another 100-star system and Kyle had developed a button we could put our belt for immediate withdrawal from a planet. He had also placed such buttons on the bridge of each of our ships. Kyle had also invented a monitor that showed other dimensions. We spent over a week just looking at the various dimensions. Then one afternoon, I told Kyle I wish we could see our kids and we began to coalesce and in a few moments; we were in my father's house. He looked up from his newspaper and he saw us. He jumped to his feet and called for my mother who hurried down the stairs and ran to us and hugged both necks. Father shook our hands and picked up the phone to let Kyle's parents know he was here and they rushed over to greet us. My father was greatly interested in this new power to coalesce and travel light years in mere seconds.

They both looked younger than they had years. Kyle's mother and dad also looked younger. Word was sent to the teachers to release our children to come home. They were in the fifth grade now and doing integrated mathematics and advanced astrogation and other subjects vastly advanced. It was nice to know that the earth scientists had been keeping pace with all the study and all the other projects that I had left unfinished at MIT. I had asked the teachers to come along and give us first-hand information as to how well our children are doing. They honored us with reports that said that in many ways the children could be teaching them. I then announced that the children would be coming with us at least the boys were, the girls were not interested, I take that back two of my girls and two of Kyle's wanted to come along and we agreed telling our mothers that we had everything that the girls would need, being girls. Both sets of parents wanted to come also for it would be lonely without the children. I told him yes, they can come as we had facilities for them also. The teachers were encouraged to use the next six months in visiting the pleasures spas and maybe take a tour of the known planets to help increase their teaching abilities. And they had their cards to cover any costs one of the planets may charge for things they would like to bring back to the classroom and their homes here in the compound.

I was glad the parents were becoming more telepathic for I felt the need of their help to keep the group together. The teachers left, and we gathered out on the patio, and I told my parents and the children to think of the coalescence and we shimmered and were gone appearing on my ship. Kids being kids, they were always hungry, and they knew where this food dispensary was, and all headed that way. The parents wanted to know when we had found the ability to coalesce and I told them about an hour ago which flabbergasted them. Then I showed them where their cabins would be at and they went in to refresh themselves.

Kyle and I retired to our cabin to discuss the coalescence. Kyle said, "Tom, it feels like it's getting stronger! Do you know what's happening to us?"

I was slow in replying, but I said this, "Kyle, my love, I think we may be on to the second plane of coalescence. Which means that we are about to meet coalescence beings. Or what they would term on earth, Angels."

Kyle responded slowly, "now that you mention it, I think you may be right. All our lives, we have lived up to the betterment of our people who just 30 years ago were in a world of torment and premeditated pain. Bad people abounded, and hate was beginning to reign supreme; until you came along and set the world on the way to A New Beginning. You showed the world how to live in peace and committed contentment by doing things that brought them joy and helped other people. By building these ships, you showed them peace came with action and you put over 10,000,000,000 people to work and it led the government to hire billions giving them a sense of self-worth. You brought peace to the world that was slowly drowning in its own tears. Which is one of the reasons why I love you so much and know without a doubt that you love me with the same depth of your being." There was a knock at the door and to my surprise nearly the whole ship was there, and they said in one voice, "God has blessed you with the power to go on to the next plane. And I think you can take as many with you that have reached this status." I immediately sent for my other four daughters or eight as four of them were Kyle's. They too began to feel the coalescence. Everyone's attire changed to white robes. I went to the bridge with Kyle and the others and through the screen you can see in the distance seven planets that had no sun and yet had light. I was about to coalesce but a voice in my head said that it was too far as yet."

The crew returned to their jobs and are gun points were sealed. Supper that night started in solemnity and ended in a happy and carefree mood. There was no meat, only fruits and vegetables some were cooked but most were in its natural state and there are fruits there that I did not recognize but were delicious and filling and joyful. After supper everything anybody did, was a blessing; for their hearts and their minds were in sync. Everyone felt a joy that spread from head to toe. When we went to bed that night we made love so deep that our minds were intertwined just as our bodies were.

The next day we passed into a realm without stars and a feeling of expectancy that they could not explain. But Kyle and I coalesced us closer to what now appeared to be huge world's that were without sunlight.

As Kyle and I dressed the next morning we could only find white robes to wear, so we just dressed in them. We went to read the night crew from the bridge. Even though the monitors indicated that we were traveling at great speed, it did not seem that we were traveling at all. I checked the controls and they were working properly, so I know you are traveling at a great speed, and our destination seemed to be the huge orange planet. Kyle spoke to me in mind, *"my love, I feel you and I give in to the stress that I feel in you for all good things come in coalesce but a voice in my head said that it was too far as yet.""* The crew returned to their jobs and are gun points were sealed. Supper that night started in solemnity and ended in a happy and carefree mood. There was no meat, only fruits and vegetables some were cooked but most were in its natural state and there are fruits there that I did not recognize but were delicious and filling and joyful. After supper everything anybody did, was a blessing; for their hearts and their minds were in sync. Everyone felt a joy that spread from head to toe. When we went to bed that night we made love so deep that our minds were intertwined just as our bodies were. The next day we passed into a realm without stars and a feeling of expectancy that they could not explain. But Kyle and I coalesced us closer to what now appeared to be huge world's that were without sunlight. As Kyle and I dressed the next morning we could only find white robes to wear, so we just dressed in them. We went to bed that night leaving the crew from the bridge. Even though the monitors indicated that we were traveling at great speed making good time. I know it feels like we're going nowhere. The monitors indicate we are moving somewhere very fast. Take time to wait, my love.* I said in response, "the monitors also show that the rest of the fleet are over 10,000 clicks behind us. Sporidian one to the fleet, tell me what you see."

Charles, currently in charge of the fleet and seeing nothing but space and stars. We can no longer detect your ship on our screens. Any further instructions?"

"No, just maintain your position. General Tom out."

After breakfast which comprised mainly of fruits and vegetables with some dipping sauces that were delicious and in themselves and there were fewer fruits that I could put a name to but were delicious nonetheless. My hunger for them had increased from the day before and yet the more we ate, the table always seemed full. When the last person left the table, it was quite clean. I went to the bridge with Kyle and the moment we got there, there appeared on the screen the huge orange planet it seemed to be larger than our sun. It was so large that you could fit over 10 Jupiter's inside it and still have room to spare.

I felt the ship coalescing to the planet and came in for a soft landing. We all exited the ship and were greeted by 40 apparent humans. They did not speak but we heard them anyway telepathically.

"Welcome my friends, welcome indeed. We have waited a long time for the crystals at last. We used the crystals to bring peace and prosperity to our planet and spread through our portion of this galaxy."

"How did you manage to enter our Tertiary field? All the other ships pass us by without detecting our presence of the tertiary field planets? And what is more, how did you do it alive? For up to now all that have come have been the dead. But you can answer these questions directly to the Michael for He wishes to see you and Kyle, your parents and your children. In fact, that is the main reason that I was sent to greet you. The members of the ship are to return to the fleet. But you will follow me for I lead you to the light that emanates from Michael himself. Please hold your questions General Tom."

Before long we stood in front of some massive doors which opened on their own accord. We immediately bowed to the PRESENCE that was the Michael. Our guide disappeared but Michael beckoned us forward.

"Live humans! I have not seen any in over 2000 years, for I am the Christ Michael. Others thought it was a mistake to go to a world so enmired in the darkness. But to test my own power I had to go to where the star had fallen. A Morning Star has not fallen in more time than you can conceive. Since this was my sector it was up to me to walk in the darkness and to spread some light for I knew you were receivable to my presence. You are the culmination of that effort and I know that from now on your plan will burn brightly and allow your people to come and see me. You have questions my son Tom, ask and I shall reveal."

"I have sought you ever since I read the Urantia book. It taught me the only way to know God was through you. Was it necessary to let us all f wallow in despair but I realized the answer without telling me that we had to climb out of the muck ourselves in order to be worthy of meeting you. Kyle and I achieved coalescence along with my parents and my innocent children and a few others that I should have brought along. But at the beginning of the journey I had no idea that we would appear in the presence Himself and I thank you for honoring us. It was my Great Plan and Kyle's resourcefulness that got us here. Now the next question is, what happens next."

The Michael spoke, and his voice was rich and melodious, "that depends upon you. You have found your way to me and you can remain if you wish or you can return to mortality that is still challenging your plan, those that do not quite believe. I believe the choice is for the two of you. All the others would return to this ship and to the fleet that is waiting for you to return and then prayed that you may return to them."

"And you will not tell me what to do for it has to come from within. I know that all of this will still be awaiting me and Kyle when we die our actual deaths and that returning will help to illuminate the path for others that do not believe strongly enough to make the journey right now. You know my answer, but I must speak it and that is why we must return. Kyle and I have a lot to do and right now there is no one capable of doing it right."

"As you say, it did have to be your choice; but I extend to you the right to return and rest when the load gets too heavy and you need rest and rehabilitation to continue. Godspeed my son." Our guide returned. We walked out of the doors and back to our ship now blazing with the light of its own. Just before Kyle and I boarded the ship, the guide placed at my feet a box of medallions and placed one around Kyle and myself and said when you coalesce, you will return. If only for a short time. It has been a pleasure to meet the two of you. Safe journey. We boarded our ship and returned to the fleet.

"There is another option; you may stay here for an unspecified period of time and really get to know the place. If you do your ship will be sent back and when you're ready to leave, you could always coalesce."

"Kyle and I will take that option."

"I am so pleased. Shall we begin?"

"Where you lead, we will follow."

"As it should be. These are the tertiary planets. When people die, they come here first. They have to go through with the rehabilitation. They have to have the evil that has seeped into them removed and unfortunately for some, it is not a painless series of extractions, for lack of a better word. Depending upon how much evil has entered them through their thoughts and their actions and the Fallen Star that has taken control of them the harder it is to cleanse the soul. If even the evilest person on earth were to turn his life around he would make his phase shorter. But that is not likely to their unfortunate being. It harms our heart when one of your people allows the Fallen Star to take more and more control of them. They do some of the most abhorrent thing's to their own people and try to make the people think that it is for their own good. One of them actually made it to the presidency of owning your most respected countries from 2016 to 2020. He will spend a hundred million years before he is himself again. He made it worse by turning everybody against each other and making it possible for children to kill their parents and the worst ones turned evil kill without compunction. Killing kids in their school, many of who were still pure at heart."

But that is still the past and the two of you keep looking toward the future, as you always have. That was what made you unique and enabled you to tap into the power of the white crystals. That is why some of your crew can coalesce, although there is not nearly as many as we had hoped, and the number is growing on a daily basis. Just one or two learned to coalesce, they can't understand the meaning of it, but given a little time; they will make it here. When the Christ Michael..."

"Clarify for me why you call him the 'Christ' Michael, if you please?"

"It is a fair question and I have received the okay to make the explanation. Your other people who can coalesce, still think that this universe is the only universe, when in truth this galaxy is only one of millions of galaxies in this universe but you have to know that there are other universes that together form what is called a 'super universe' and then you reach Paradise but you have to travel these tertiary planets and learn much of what you do not know. But in the case of you two, that journey will be much easier because you _know_ that there is more to live and to learn and do it with an open heart and a clear mind unclouded by doubt. And face what is coming with the anxiety of longing. I digress, back to your original question, in every 10 galaxies there has to be someone who looks after those quintillions of spirits that reside in every sentient being regardless of their shape, size, color, sexual orientation, or species; in time, they will have their own Tom and Kyle. But for most of them, it will be a long hard road to travel because they were pleased to believe what their heart tells them.

"The two of you have embraced the concept to a point very uncommon in any universe for those that breathe air. I don't know if you noticed, but you are not breathing. Drink this." It tasted so wonderful as to defy description in the human language. "That will refresh you for a period of time keeping your bodily functions functioning. Now back to what I was saying, is that there is a 'Christ Michael' that governs 1,000 galaxies and the reason we called him 'Christ' is because when a new 1,000nth galaxy is made and populated, God the Father, God the Son and the Infinite Spirit, conjoin to produce a new 'Christ' from the Michael hierarchy. Produced primarily by the thoughts of Jesus Christ, the corps of Michael's produce a new soul that is sparkling clean and totally without evil." It was a long time and will probably be longer still sense a Michael Fell. Not far mind you, but he did entertain some evil thoughts which made the evil in his sector stronger and harder to be rid of. I am told now, that you will be allowed to sleep one night in heaven, before you return to your ship and continue to spread the word of God through your thoughts and actions.

That does not apply to sex, for it is a needful thing. We were surprised and pleased when you and Kyle impregnated those 200 women without sex. Your children are born without that trace of evil that most sex has, when it is done by bad or even marginally bad people. When you and Kyle started your great project, so much of your world was drowning in the dark side. What you put in place makes it harder for the Fallen Star to turn people to the dark side. It makes those, even the evilest, now begin to think good thoughts because they see nothing but good around them and they feel the good thoughts of the people surrounding them and choking the evil out. Ever nudging them to do right rather than wrong. Murders on your planet used to run rampant and millions of innocent people died at the hands of the evildoers. I will let you sleep now. We kissed with a loving and longing and made the Love that could have lasted a lifetime. Then we slept. When we awoke, our guide was still there, and he said, "Oh! To be human and as pure as the two of you are. God himself has loved you and you are blessed. You must endure after the Tertiary System, comes the secondary and the primary lifetimes. But now it is time for you to coalesce back to your ship. Now, and Kyle and I felt ourselves beginning to coalesce and we said goodbye for now, but there is much we must do" and with that we disappeared and reappeared on our ship. Our parents embraced us, and they could feel the new love that resides in us. Then we went to our quarters. As we walked to our quarters, we could see the heads turn for we were part of our small force in robes. All of our clothing had been changed into robes. It made us know how to spot the others that could coalesce.

We began to have meetings with these men and they became less self-conscious about their robes. I brought out the Urantia book and replicated more copies so that each man had one and could read it at his leisure.

The next morning, I announced to the crew of all 1000 ships to stand ready for an inspection. What we were looking for were those in robes and we soon had so many at our meetings that we moved on to large conference hall that was unique to my ship, now I know why I wanted it. After the inspection I announced that we were returning to the rest of our fleet. Where Kyle and I held another inspection of the ships and we seemed to be gliding rather than walking but our robes covered our feet, so it was hard to say. The inspection of 2 million men turned up only 100,000 in robes; which was a bit of a disappointment, "but not really" raced through our minds.

But when we inspected this one species, I knew they were the hope, Kyle and I was going to witness the second coming of the special one, The Christ Michael, himself. I stood as everyone else did and before the Christ Michael. It seems everyone wanted to be here especially, the Archangels. It was always that way because they are the pool to be chosen from and embraced by God the Father, God the Son, and God the Eternal Spirit and blessed by the trio, he will not fail again. 200 God's and Goddesses-from which are picked, those that would be made a Michael; the trumpet blew and a choir began a beautiful song of peace and contentment of the brotherhood of mankind all of which are the same thing when coalesce of a person takes place. The 100,000 men and/or women that had coalesced many times their robes changed to a bright green and I can only guess that it was a greater power, that change the color of each group of humans as they moved about and made straight areas by making groups in line by color, that they originated with — from The Adamic Beginning — and wore proudly before Him as he passes all of us as he walks towards His massive Throne as he makes his way, He stops and turns toward us and walked toward him by the quantity of the color our group that is the largest and He raises His mighty hands he reaches toward them, one at a time, and they became Angels.

With all the others made into Angels, Kyle and I just stood there looking at Him we were hit by something more than telepathy. We Just **_Knew_** that we were to follow Him as He stepped the three steps to the Throne where He sat, and Kyle and I stopped and bowed to Him. Again, we did not hear through our ears; rather it seemed to be part of us. He Said to us, everyone should now be introduced to Tom Raymond and to Kyle Harkness, the first humans to ever reach Tertia still alive. I have granted them this favor because of it. For a short period of time I shall become a human being, once again. That is when I found my voice and drop to one knee as did Kyle, and I said, "we will be honored to accompany Your Presence as He walks the earth for the first time in over 2000 years. But My Lord, why have Kyle and I remained alive?" Again, the answer was everywhere, and He responded "the two of you are living proof that homosexuals can and do love each other with all their heart, their mind, their body, and their soul. They have shown the rightness of the heart and of the brain that produce the fact that true love brings us closer together, spiritually.

"So, they will be returned to earth with Me.

The End

Printed in the United States
By Bookmasters